MEAN STREAK

**Other books in
The Kids from Kennedy Middle School series**

The Kids From
KENNEDY MIDDLE SCHOOL

MEAN STREAK

ILENE COOPER

MORROW JUNIOR BOOKS
NEW YORK

Printed in the United States of America.
1   2   3   4   5   6   7   8   9   10
Library of Congress Cataloging-in-Publication Data
Cooper, Ilene.
Mean streak / Ilene Cooper.
p.   cm.—(The Kids from Kennedy Middle School)
Summary: Having alienated her best friend Robin, eleven-year-old
Veronica has no one to turn to for sympathy and support when it
appears that her divorced father might remarry.
ISBN 0-688-08431-1
[1. Friendship—Fiction.   2. Remarriage—Fiction.]   I. Title.
II. Series: Cooper, Ilene.   Kids from Kennedy Middle School.
PZ7.C7856Me   1991
[Fic]—dc20   90–28103   CIP   AC

For my two mothers,
Lillian Friedman Cooper
and
Judith Nahamkin Seid

MEAN STREAK

CHAPTER
ONE

Veronica Volner narrowed her eyes. "Look who's here."

Candy Dahl, Veronica's best friend, put down her milk shake and turned around. Robin Miller was walking through the door of The Hut, Forest Glen's local hamburger hangout. Sharon Anderson and Gretchen Hubbard were right behind her.

"I can't believe that Robin is hanging around with Gretchen Hippopotamus," Candy said, turning back to her milk shake. "She must really be hard up."

Veronica tossed her dark hair over her shoulder. "She must be desperate."

Taking a sip of her cola, Veronica watched as Robin, Sharon, and Gretchen made their way through the maze of rickety tables and walked up to the counter to order.

Despite what she'd said, Veronica felt a pang when she saw Robin laughing with Gretchen and Sharon. For a long time, she and Robin had been best friends. It all seemed so silly now, their argument over Jonathan Rossi. Veronica had wanted to ask him to a party, but he liked Robin better. Veronica hadn't really cared at all about Jonathan. She just wanted to go with him because he was one of the few sixth-grade boys taller than she was.

Now, she wished she had never started the whole stupid business. Though she never would have admitted it, she missed Robin. Veronica pretty much ran the sixth-grade girls, but none of them was as much fun as Robin.

Veronica turned back to Candy. "So when are you leaving for your grandmother's?" she asked.

Candy rolled her blue Kewpie doll eyes. "We were supposed to drive down tomorrow, but my mother is so disorganized. She hasn't finished her Christmas shopping, so we probably won't go until the next day. At least it will be warm in Florida."

"It will probably rain," Veronica said. She didn't like the idea of Candy's spending Christmas break lounging around a pool in Florida while she was going to be stuck in Forest Glen, Illinois. Usually, her mother planned something special for vacations, but this year Mrs. Volner's job at an advertising agency was keeping her very busy. Getting away was out of the question.

Candy pouted a little at Veronica's prediction, but, as usual, she finally agreed with her. "Well, it might rain, but we're going to Disney World anyway."

"Disney World's all right. Little kids like it, I guess." Veronica's voice was iced with boredom.

"Hi, Veronica." Veronica looked up, to see Lisa Weissmann standing in front of her. "Hi, Candy," Lisa added a little belatedly.

"Sit down," Veronica said, patting the seat next to her.

"I called your house. Your housekeeper said you were here."

Veronica made a small face. "I wish there was someplace more interesting to go."

"My dad's going to take me shopping downtown tomorrow." "Downtown" was downtown Chicago, about a half-hour's drive away.

"That's not much better," Veronica said listlessly. Her mother worked in Chicago, and her father lived there in a high-rise condominium that had a wraparound view of Lake Michigan. She got to see plenty of Chicago.

"Guess what?" Lisa said, leaning forward.

"What?" Veronica asked.

"My parents decided we should go away. We're going to go to New York the day after Christmas."

It seemed to Veronica that everyone was deserting her. Another friend, Jessica Moriarity, had already left on a cruise. "I'm glad I'm going to be home," she finally said.

"Why?" Lisa asked.

Trying to look innocent, Veronica said, "Oh, Billy . . ." She let her voice trail off, leaving the girls to fill in the blanks.

"Billy's so cute," Candy said with a sigh. "And the star of the basketball team, too."

The Kennedy Middle School basketball team hadn't been doing very well until Billy Page joined it. Billy was not only a good player, he was even taller than Jonathan. He and Veronica had gone to a holiday dance at the community center last Saturday, but implying that they had plans for Christmas vacation wasn't strictly true. When he had taken Veronica home after the dance, he had told her he would call her soon.

"Are you going to see Billy?" Lisa asked with interest.

Veronica waved her hand vaguely. "We haven't decided exactly what we're going to do yet."

"You have all the luck," Lisa said enviously. "Billy only moved here a couple of months ago, and you've already got him all tied up."

Veronica brightened. She liked being the center of attention, and she usually was. Even if she was going to have to stay home during Christmas vacation, she would make sure that something fun happened.

"Are you going to order?" she asked Lisa.

"Nope. I really just came to find you."

"Well, let's get out of here. I still have a little Christmas shopping left to do."

"All right," Lisa agreed.

Candy dutifully took a few last slurps of her milk shake and got up.

As the girls walked toward the door, Veronica cast a baleful glance at Robin and her friends. She leaned toward Lisa and Candy and whispered conspiratorially, "The three blind mice." Gratified by Lisa's and Candy's laughter, she improvised, "Make that two blind mice and one little pig."

That broke the girls up even more.

"Gretchen is a little pig, all right." Lisa giggled.

"Did you see what she was eating?" Candy asked as they stepped outside into the cold air.

"A hot dog and brownie on a bun?" Veronica suggested.

"A salad."

"Maybe she's on a diet," Lisa said.

"Well, it's about time if she is." Veronica pulled her mittens out of her coat pocket.

"She could certainly stand to lose a few pounds," Candy added righteously.

Veronica exchanged a sly glance with Lisa. Candy, with her blue eyes and blond hair, was cute enough, but she was far from slim. She could stand to lose a few pounds herself.

Candy caught their look. "Hey, Gretchen's huge. You can't compare me—"

"We didn't say anything, did we, Lisa?" Veronica said virtuously.

"No, we didn't," Lisa replied with a smirk.

"But, Candy . . ."

"What?"

"I'd lay off the candy if I were you." Veronica laughed.

"Ha, ha," Candy said, but she nervously adjusted her coat as if trying to cover up some of the offending pounds.

Forest Glen was a quaint little town with a number of shops. There were several clothing boutiques that had the latest in sweatshirts and jeans and jewelry. A bookstore and a couple of antiques stores were also likely spots to look for Christmas gifts. Candy remembered she had to buy something for her grandmother, so Veronica and Lisa agreed to go with her to Celeste's, which had a good selection of earrings.

"I can't believe your grandmother wears earrings," Lisa said as they wandered past one counter filled with belts and gloves and another loaded with purses.

"Why shouldn't she?" Candy asked, stopping at a display of dangling, brightly colored pierced earrings.

"Isn't she too old for that kind of stuff?"

"You don't stop wearing jewelry just because you get old."

Veronica held up the hand mirror sitting on the counter and peered at herself intently. Privately, she often wavered in her feelings about the way she looked. Her long dark hair was thick and shiny, and her brown eyes, though ordinary, had nice flecks of green in them. But her nose was a little too long and her face rather thin. Nevertheless, Veronica had realized long ago that it wasn't so much the way you looked as how other people perceived you. Veronica knew everyone thought she was attractive and cool, because that's how she acted. It was like performing. The audience might know you were playing a part, but if you were good enough, they believed you anyway.

"I know what Lisa means," Veronica said, putting down the mirror. "Why bother putting on makeup or wearing jewelry when you get old? Who cares?"

Candy looked surprised. "I suppose my grandmother does," she answered.

After examining all of Celeste's earrings, Candy decided there was nothing there that she liked. "Maybe a scarf," she muttered.

"This is getting boring, Candy. What do *you* have to buy?" Lisa asked Veronica.

"Just one present," Veronica replied shortly.

"Who's it for?" Candy wanted to know.

"Sandy."

Sandy was her father's new girlfriend. Veronica hated her. The Volners had been divorced for a couple of years and her father had had other girlfriends before, but no one like Sandy. For one thing, she was young—too young. Veronica didn't know her age exactly, but she looked a lot younger than Veronica's mother. And she made Mr. Volner act young, even though he was just a regular middle-aged man. Veronica cringed when she saw her father with Sandy, whispering, laughing, and touching each other the way the kids in high school did.

Then there was the matter of Sandy's attitude toward her. She was friendly enough, but she didn't seem to understand the special place that Veronica had in her father's life—or at least wanted to have. Mr. Volner was a busy lawyer, and sometimes he had to cancel plans. Veronica was always disappointed when that happened, even though her father usually had a good excuse. If Sandy was going to be hanging around, Veronica wanted her to know that she was important, too. She had seen plenty of TV shows where the father's girlfriend tries to win over his child. Sandy didn't seem very interested in trying to win her over. She smiled and made conversation, but her attention was always on Veronica's father.

Mr. Volner, however, really wanted Veronica and Sandy to be friends. A few weeks ago he had slipped Veronica twenty dollars and asked her to be sure to buy Sandy "a little something," as he put it. Veronica had promised her father she would get Sandy a nice gift, but Christmas was only a couple of days away, and Veronica hadn't even bothered to look for anything that Sandy might like.

"What are you going to get her?" Lisa asked as they walked outside.

"I'm not sure," Veronica said. "She's so great-looking, she could wear anything."

As they strolled down the street, Veronica told the girls how great Sandy was. It was important to Veronica that nobody know how she really felt about Sandy. Veronica liked people to think that everything in her life was perfect. If her father had to have a girlfriend, then she was going to be perfect, too.

"She works on a magazine, right?" Lisa asked.

"Yes. She's a writer."

"What magazine?" Candy asked.

Veronica hesitated. It was a business magazine. The things Sandy wrote about—the stock market and banking—sounded extremely boring to Veronica, but she only shrugged and said, "You probably haven't heard of it." Veronica wanted to make Candy think she was too dumb to recognize the name of the magazine, though actually, Veronica had trouble remembering it herself. "She writes about financial matters." This was a phrase she had heard Sandy use. "She even interviewed someone at the White House once."

Candy looked impressed, but Lisa just said, "So what are you going to get her?"

They were right in front of the bookstore. Veronica stopped, peered inside, and said, "Maybe I can find something in here."

Once inside, Veronica stood in the middle of the store, looking around. There were books everywhere: cookbooks, biographies, even a whole rack of dictionaries. Over in the corner, on a table covered with a lace tablecloth, there was a huge display of the latest book by romance writer Laine Leslie. It was called *Passion Point*.

Lisa marched over to the table, gingerly took one off the pile, and leafed through it. "Come here," she said, motioning Veronica and Candy over. "Check this out."

Veronica began reading aloud, though she kept her voice at a whisper. " 'Michael ran his hand through Dinah's long dark hair. Then he clutched her to him and started trailing kisses down her neck. One hand—' "

"May I help you?" A salesman with a large Adam's apple and horn-rimmed glasses looked down at the girls with a frown.

Veronica slammed the book shut and hurriedly placed it back on the table, almost tumbling over the display. "Just looking," Veronica said, and turned toward the dictionaries.

"Why don't you buy Sandy *Passion Point?*" Candy asked eagerly. "It sounds really good."

"No, not *Passion Point.*" The last thing Veronica wanted to do was give Sandy any further ideas about romance. Instead, she picked up one of the heavy, boring-looking dictionaries. Sandy was a writer, so she probably already had a dictionary. Flipping the book over, Veronica saw that it was on sale for only $11.95. If she bought it, she could probably keep the change. "I think I'll get this," Veronica announced. Who cared whether Sandy already had one? It would seem like a thoughtful gift.

Candy looked disappointed. "She'd probably like *Passion Point* better."

True enough, Veronica thought. That's why she's getting the dictionary. "This makes a statement," Veronica informed Candy. She wondered whether Sandy would understand the statement: Spend more time working, and stay away from my dad.

After Veronica made her purchase, the girls

did a little more shopping before Candy called her mother to drive them home. Candy and Lisa lived just down the street from each other in the same development. Veronica's house was nearby but in a posher part of town near Lake Michigan, so Mrs. Dahl dropped Veronica off first.

Although it was only about five o'clock, it was already dark. Veronica's large brick house was dark inside, too, except for a light coming from the kitchen. Veronica supposed that Helen, the Volners' housekeeper, was straightening up in there before she headed home.

Veronica flicked on a light in the hall, and another one in the elegant living room. Then she walked into the kitchen.

"Hi, Helen," Veronica said, opening the door of the refrigerator, barely glancing at the woman who was scouring the sink.

"Veronica, your father called."

"He did?" Veronica said, suddenly paying attention.

Helen turned on the water full blast, and Veronica had to strain to hear her. "Said he'd call you back."

Veronica headed toward the phone. "I'll call him."

Shaking her head, Helen said, "Not home. Told me he was going out for a while and he'd catch you at suppertime."

Veronica knew full well her father would never call dinner suppertime, nor would he use the phrase *catch you;* but whatever Helen's other faults, she usually got the gist of a phone message. Veronica went back to the refrigerator, rummaged through the shelves, and finally pulled out the Coca-Cola.

"Helen, there was much better food around here when Alex was home."

Helen snorted and placed the scouring pad she was using on the edge of the sink. "When your brother was home, we never had any food in the house at all. He'd eat it as fast as I could make it. Bet he's not getting fat on that British cooking," Helen added. Alex was spending his junior year at college as an exchange student in England.

"You baked a lot more when he was home, too," Veronica said accusingly.

"Your mother gave me strict instructions not to do any baking," Helen retorted. "Watching her figure."

Veronica didn't doubt that, even though her mother was as skinny as a model. In fact, she looked rather like a model—tall, with dark hair like Veronica's, but swept into an elegant twist. Veronica's mother, an account executive at an advertising agency, was always telling Veronica that looking your best was important. Whatever other problems Veronica had with her mother, she had to admit that Mrs. Volner always looked her best.

Pulling a bag of chips out of the cupboard and ignoring Helen's scowl as a few crumbs fell, Veronica pulled out a chair and sat down at the kitchen table. "What time is my mother coming home?"

Helen glanced at the watch on the frayed band that circled her skinny wrist. "Should have been home by now."

Veronica drank some of her cola, then pushed it away. Mrs. Volner had said she'd be home from the office early for once because business was slow during the holiday season. Usually, she didn't arrive until almost seven.

As if on cue, Mrs. Volner opened the front door and called, "Hello, everyone, I'm home."

"So much for quality time, Mother," Veronica said in a disparaging voice as Mrs. Volner walked into the kitchen.

A small, hurt look crossed Mrs. Volner's face—one that Veronica had hoped she'd elicit by her comment. As soon as she saw her mother's mouth turn down, however, Veronica felt bad.

"Don't mind Veronica," Helen said, taking them both in with a shrewd glance. "She just got home a few minutes ago herself."

Big mouth, Veronica thought, but all she said was, "I might have come home earlier if I'd really thought you'd be here."

"I'm here now," Mrs. Volner said, trying to appear cheerful. "Let's decide what we're going to do about dinner."

"There's leftover turkey in the fridge," Helen said sourly as she walked to the hall closet to get her coat. "See you tomorrow."

Veronica tried to decide whether it was worth it to prolong her mother's discomfiture. Deciding it wasn't, she said, "I'm tired of turkey. Maybe we could get a pizza."

"Good idea," Mrs. Volner said in a hearty voice. She took off her coat. "Would you like to go to a movie later?"

Veronica shrugged. She had asked Lisa and Candy whether they wanted to come to her house for a sleepover, but both of them were tied up with family plans. "A movie sounds okay."

"Fine, I'll check the paper."

"We can't leave until Daddy calls back."

Mrs. Volner had stepped into the hallway, so Veronica couldn't see her face, but the hard tone in her mother's voice was familiar as she said, "Your father phoned?"

"Helen said he'd call back around dinner."

Mrs. Volner came back into the kitchen and sat down at the table across from Veronica. "I suppose he wants to make some plans for Christmas Day. You're supposed to spend half the day with him."

As if she didn't know. Holidays had been nothing but a tug-of-war ever since the divorce. Either Veronica had to share the day with both parents, having a good time with neither of them, or she alternated holidays and spent the day listening to one parent complain about the other. Some fun.

Noting the look on Veronica's face, her mother sighed and said, "Maybe I'll just take a nap until it's time to eat. Go ahead and call for the pizza whenever you're hungry."

After her mother went upstairs, Veronica was at loose ends. She thought about calling Kim Chapman or Natalie Wolk, but she didn't want to tie up the telephone line and miss her father's call. Finally, she went to her room to listen to her Walkman.

It was a very nice room, thanks to her mother's flair for decorating. A canopied bed was the focal point, and the rose-decorated fabric of the spread matched the wallpaper, where rosebuds trailed on green vines. An antique dresser with a carved mirror stood in the corner, and there was a rocking chair near the window that overlooked the garden. Sometimes Veronica told her mother that she wished she could redo her room, get rid of all floral prints and go for a more modern look. The truth was, though, she really felt safe here.

Flopping down on her bed, Veronica fumbled under the pillow for her cassette player. She kept it there in case she wanted to hear some music before she went to bed. Adjusting the earphones, she listened to a Jawbreakers tape for a while until she heard the phone ringing through the pounding beat of the guitars and drums.

Fortunately, Mrs. Volner had gotten her a long-requested telephone for her last birthday, so Veronica was able to reach over to the end table and pick up the receiver.

"Veronica, sweetie, it's your old man." Mr. Volner's upbeat voice came over the line.

"Hi, Daddy," Veronica said, curling herself into a little ball. "What's up?"

"Well, some fun, I hope, if your mother agrees."

"What kind of fun?"

"Sandy and I are going to Snow Trail Lodge for a little skiing after Christmas, and we want you to join us."

Veronica was torn. A ski lodge sounded neat, and she wanted to spend time with her father, but Sandy's presence would ruin everything. "Couldn't we just go together? The two of us?"

"Veronica, I want you and Sandy to get better acquainted."

Do we have to? Veronica thought to herself, but all she said to her father was, "I'm not sure Mom will let me go."

"I know I'll have to make special arrangements with her, but I hoped if I talked to you first, you could tell her how much you wanted to join us."

So here she was, stuck in the middle as usual. If she pushed for the ski lodge, her mother would be mad; if she didn't, her father would be disappointed.

"Well, I'll ask her," Veronica said after a moment. "But you're the one who has to set things up."

"Sure, of course. Just soften her up a little.

Talk to her tonight, and I'll give her a call tomorrow."

"Okay, Daddy."

"Swell. We'll have a good time, honey."

After she hung up, Veronica rolled over and stared at the ceiling. She could hear the sound of her mother stirring in her bedroom across the hall. Talking her mother into this trip wasn't going to be easy. Veronica wondered whether the fun her father promised would be worth the effort.

CHAPTER
TWO

"Veronica! Get up, you sleepyhead. It's time to hit the slopes."

Veronica opened one eye, saw Sandy standing in the doorway carrying a fuchsia ski suit and purple hat, and turned over.

Moving briskly, Sandy walked over to the bed and gave her a shake. "Veronica, if you want to have some breakfast before we get out there . . ."

She's not going to leave, Veronica thought to herself. Slowly, she sat up and rubbed her eyes. "Sandy, I don't want to go skiing this morning."

"You don't?" Sandy asked with surprise.

"I'm sore all over. I've had enough."

She had had enough yesterday and even the

day before. This was turning into the longest weekend of Veronica's life.

It was difficult now for Veronica to believe that she actually had pleaded with her mother to let her come. Mrs. Volner had been negative about the idea right from the first.

"No, Veronica," she had said, looking down at the cheese congealing on her pizza that night at dinner after Mr. Volner's call, "I don't think so."

"But why not?" Veronica pouted.

"Your father knows he's supposed to give me two weeks' notice if he wants to take you out of the city. He's telling me barely four days in advance."

"Great. This is about you and Daddy then, not about what I'd like to do."

"He's supposed to stick to the rules," Mrs. Volner said stubbornly.

"Maybe he only thought of it at the last minute."

"I doubt it."

Veronica looked at her mother shrewdly. "You don't want me to go because Sandy will be along."

"That's part of it," Mrs. Volner admitted. "If it was just the two of you that would be one thing—"

"Oh, Mother," Veronica groaned, "don't be so old-fashioned."

"I hardly consider myself old-fashioned," Mrs. Volner said, her expression tight.

At that moment, Veronica felt a little sorry for her mother, because she understood how it felt not to want Sandy around. Even so, she had decided she wasn't going to let the opportunity to have some time with her father slip away. Putting on her saddest expression, Veronica said, "I don't get to see Daddy that often. You said yourself you wished I could spend more time with him."

Mrs. Volner suddenly looked very tired. "I know you miss your father, Veronica. Things haven't been the same since he left . . . for any of us."

Veronica never did understand what had gone wrong with her parents' marriage. There hadn't been much fighting, at least not in front of her. One day, when Veronica was almost nine, Mr. Volner had called her and Alex into the den and told them he wasn't happy and that he was moving out.

Alex had taken the news with stony silence, but Veronica had cried and asked whether her father meant that he wasn't happy with her. Mr. Volner had assured her that this wasn't the case, that the bad feelings were strictly between him and Veronica's mother. He wouldn't tell her more than that. When Veronica pressed her mother for answers, Mrs. Volner simply said, "Sometimes things don't work out."

Alex had guessed that there was another woman in their father's life. As nearly as Veronica could tell, though, there were lots of other women; Mr. Volner was always dating once he took an apartment in downtown Chicago. While Alex was still home, Veronica felt she had an ally. He could handle all the emotions swirling around their house far better than she could, and Veronica certainly admired the way Alex treated their father—with a cold disdain that she never could muster.

However, soon after the divorce, Alex had left for college, and Veronica was desolate. Alex had told her to phone him whenever she needed to talk, and she had. Now that he was in England, she had to make do with writing letters and a weekly call. With her mother on the extension, there was plenty of newsy chit-chat but precious little time for truth.

Veronica wished Alex had been around to advise her about the ski trip. After Veronica's torrent of tears, Mrs. Volner finally had given in and agreed that Veronica could go. Alex probably would have been smart enough to figure out that the whole thing was going to be a disaster from start to finish.

Sandy eyed Veronica distastefully. "What do you mean, you don't want to ski this morning?"

Veronica sat up a little straighter. "Skiing isn't as much fun as I thought it would be. It's boring."

"Come on, Veronica, I know you're not a natural on the slopes, but with a little more work, you might get the hang of it."

"I haven't had that much trouble," Veronica said indignantly.

"Your father and I have watched you on the bunny hill. You can hardly stay up on your skis."

Veronica was horribly embarrassed, but she didn't want Sandy to know that. "I don't think the instructor is very good."

Before Sandy could retort, Mr. Volner stepped through the open doorway. Tall, with hair just starting to turn gray, Mr. Volner was an impressive figure. When he walked into a room, it was as if a light had been turned on— at least it seemed that way to Veronica. "What are you doing in bed, sweetie?" Mr. Volner asked.

Veronica's aplomb faded away quickly. "I . . . I'm not feeling that well, Daddy."

Sandy rolled her eyes.

"Well, I'm *not*," Veronica said defensively. "My whole body hurts."

Her father walked over and kissed her on the top of the head. "I know, but we'll jump in the whirlpool later. The more time you spend on the slopes, the sooner you'll gain some confidence."

"That's just what I told her, Neal," Sandy said, pleased.

"We're going down to the dining room," Mr. Volner told Veronica. "Meet us down there as soon as you can." Putting his arm around Sandy's shoulder, he led her out of the room and shut the door.

Veronica furiously threw off her covers, got out of bed, and headed for the bathroom. She might have to go skiing, but she didn't have to hurry.

After dressing as slowly as she could in her new black ski pants and emerald green turtleneck, Veronica grabbed her jacket, hat, and gloves and went downstairs.

Under different circumstances, she knew

she might have enjoyed the Snow Trail Lodge. The huge rustic building had several stone fireplaces, where roaring flames helped create an atmosphere of coziness and charm. Although the original lodge had been built a number of years ago, many modern improvements had been added. A health club and a swimming pool took up the whole west wing, and a game room was nearby. The dining room had a sleek, sophisticated look that was in contrast to the ruggedness of the rest of the building.

Veronica stood at the entrance of the dining room, trying to find her father's table. It took her a moment because the room was so full. Then she spotted them. Sandy and her dad were in the corner, laughing together over their coffee. They looked as if they were in a world completely and utterly their own.

Veronica hesitated a moment, hoping her father would look up and see her. Then she took a breath and walked over to them. She pulled her chair out and sat down.

"Well, you finally made it," Mr. Volner said. "I ordered for you to save time."

Veronica made a face at the scrambled eggs chilling on her plate. "I don't like scrambled eggs," she said.

"Eat them anyway," Sandy said curtly.

"If you had gotten here earlier, you could have picked something yourself," Mr. Volner reproved her.

Veronica picked up her fork and started pushing the food around on her plate.

"If you don't eat something, you're not going to have enough energy to ski," Mr. Volner said.

"I don't ski anyway. All we do is walk around while that stupid instructor yells 'Keep moving.' "

"Veronica, what's the problem?" Mr. Volner asked, a frown creasing his brows. "You're not even trying to have fun."

"How can I? I freeze all day; then we come back here and go in the whirlpool. Then we eat dinner. Bor-ing."

Sandy gestured around the dining room. "There are plenty of young people here. They all seem to be having a good time."

"That's because they're here with their real families," Veronica burst out.

Sandy blushed as red as her strawberry blond hair, while Mr. Volner's frown deepened. Finally, he said, "I'm sorry you feel that way, Veronica. I thought this trip would be a good chance for you and Sandy to get to know each other better, but obviously you don't want to do that."

Veronica hated it when her father got upset with her. When her mother was angry, Veronica became very silent. This usually intimidated Mrs. Volner, until she wound up apologizing for whatever had caused their fight. Veronica knew that kind of behavior didn't work with her dad. She didn't want to back down, but the stern look on her father's face was more than Veronica felt she could take. Why had she even tried to be honest with him?

"Sorry," she muttered. "I guess I just don't like skiing as much as I thought I would."

"Well, Neal," Sandy said, finally breaking the silence, "if Veronica doesn't want to ski, maybe we shouldn't make her."

Veronica was surprised to hear a measure of support coming from Sandy.

Mr. Volner took a sip of his coffee. "Would you like to hang around the lodge today, Veronica?"

"Yes. Yes, I would."

"I don't especially like the idea of you just watching television."

"I could write some postcards." Veronica was improvising. "And I could swim."

Shrugging, Mr. Volner said, "If that's what you'd prefer."

"It is. Thank you," she added, including Sandy as she mustered a smile.

When breakfast was over, she said a bright good-bye to Sandy and her father and wandered down to the gift shop. But once she was alone, Veronica realized that staying at the lodge was just as tedious as being out on the slopes. The only advantage was that it was warmer. After surveying every item in the store, from key chains to goggles, she bought a few postcards and took them back to her room.

Flopping down on her freshly made bed, Veronica began writing cards. To Candy and Lisa, she described the lodge and mentioned how many cute boys were staying there. This was true, but most of them were in their teens and hadn't paid the least little bit of attention to her. She sent one to Jessica, even though it wouldn't arrive until after she came back from the Caribbean. Then Veronica debated about sending a card to Billy. She was mad at him; but finally, she decided to write, if only to let him know that she was having fun without him.

To Alex, Veronica wrote the truth. She had to cramp her handwriting to fit everything on the card. She didn't know how much postage it would take to get to England, so she'd have to wait and mail it from home. Still, writing down how horrible the vacation was, and how much she hated Sandy with her soft curls and honeyed voice, made Veronica feel better.

When she was done with her postcards, Veronica took the remote control from her nightstand and turned on the television. She had told her father she wouldn't spend the day in front of the tube, but the truth was that she didn't feel like getting wet in the pool any more than she wanted snow dripping down her back. Maybe she'd go swimming after lunch. The day stretched endlessly before her.

Veronica flicked from one station to another, finally landing on a talk show, where the topic was broken friendships. Getting more comfortable, she watched as a heavily made-up young woman wearing too much jewelry described how her former best friend had stolen her boyfriend. Sort of like me and Robin, Veronica thought. And just as the woman on the talk show was now saying, the worst part was that she didn't care about the guy anymore, but she really missed her best friend.

There was nobody like Robin, Veronica admitted to herself. She was funny, but she could give good advice, too. When the Volners had gotten their divorce, Robin and Alex were the only ones she could talk to.

Veronica remembered a time right after the divorce had finally gone through. She had spent the day with Candy, Lisa, and Robin, trying to make a joke out of the whole thing. "Look at it this way," Veronica had said, "I'll get twice the Christmas and birthday presents. Why, my father will probably give me presents for no reason at all." Candy and Lisa had accepted her rationalizations, but not Robin.

After the other girls had gone home, Robin had studied her carefully. "Why do you do that?"

"What?"

"Pretend you don't care."

"I don't," Veronica said flippantly.

"Oh, yes you do. I'd be miserable if my parents were getting a divorce, and I know you feel the same way."

Veronica could feel the tears welling up behind her eyes. Angrily, she turned away from Robin, but she was stopped by Robin's soft voice. "It's okay if you cry."

"I'm not crying," she responded automatically, even as the tears began running down her cheeks.

"If you feel like crying, that's what you should do."

For the first time since her father left, Veronica allowed herself to give in to all the sad emotions that were stuck inside of her. She wasn't even embarrassed when Robin handed her a crumpled tissue from her own pocket. After she was finished crying, neither of them had said another word about it.

Now, Robin seemed to want to spend her time with Sharon and that dork Gretchen Hubbard. As far as Veronica was concerned, well, that was Robin's problem. She certainly wasn't going to be the one to make the first move toward a reconciliation.

There was a time when she thought they might make up. The girls had gotten mad at Veronica and were ready to be friends with Robin again. Robin had had a chance to cause all sorts of trouble for Veronica, but she didn't. Veronica had hoped they could start over. That hadn't happened, though, and now they seemed just as far apart as ever. As she had so many times since their upset, Veronica pushed Robin from her mind.

Veronica shut off the television. What now? she wondered. There was a game room off the lobby. Maybe something was going on down there.

The room was empty except for a little boy about seven or eight. "Hey," he asked hopefully, "want to play Ninja Warriors?"

"No," Veronica answered. She might be bored, but she wasn't ready to play video games with a kid yet.

Walking over to a pinball machine, Veronica fished around in her pocket and pulled out some change. She wasn't very good at pinball, and in just a few moments the game was over.

"My turn," a voice said over her shoulder.

Veronica turned and saw standing behind her one of the teenage boys she had noticed around the lodge. Moving out of the way, Veronica let the boy step up to the pinball machine and put in his money.

With intense concentration, he began working the flippers. Bells rang and lights went off all over the machine. This guy is good, Veronica thought with admiration.

He played a long time, racking up his score before he finally shot his last ball. After adding a few more points to his total, his turn was over. That's when he noticed Veronica. "Want to play a game?" he asked.

Veronica hesitated. "I won't be much competition," she admitted.

The boy shrugged. "It's better than playing alone."

"All right." Veronica put some money into the machine. She prayed she wouldn't humiliate herself, but she wasn't very good. The boy's turns seemed to last forever, but Veronica's balls slid down the gutter almost as soon as she shot them out.

When it was finally over, the boy nodded at Veronica and left the game room. Oh well, Veronica thought, at least it would be something to tell the girls when she got home. A high school boy had challenged her to a game of pinball.

Veronica never thought she'd be eager for her father and Sandy to reappear, but she held off on lunch, hoping they'd come back to see how she was doing. Then maybe they could eat together and go to a movie somewhere. When Mr. Volner and Sandy hadn't appeared by two, Veronica figured that they must have eaten at the little café at the top of the slopes. She got a hamburger at the snack bar, and when she couldn't think of one more thing to do, she went back to her room and took a nap.

She was awakened by her father shaking her shoulder.

Rubbing the sleep out of her eyes, Veronica sat up. "Hi, Daddy. How was your skiing?"

Mr. Volner turned on the bedside lamp, causing Veronica to squint. "We had fun. How about you?"

"It was okay. I played some pinball."

"That's all?"

"I wrote postcards. And I ate."

Mr. Volner looked at her with concern. "I'm sorry you're not having a better time, sweetie."

"It's okay," Veronica said slowly, "but I wish it could have been just you and me."

"Veronica, you're not giving Sandy a chance." Mr. Volner sighed.

"She doesn't like me."

"Of course she does. I know this is hard for you, but it's important to me that you make friends with Sandy."

Veronica didn't like the sound of this. None of his other girlfriends had been around long enough to become friends.

"I guess you'll be glad to be going home tomorrow."

"Sort of," Veronica said.

Mr. Volner shook his head. "You're going to have to come to some kind of accommodation with Sandy. You know, since the divorce I haven't been the sort of dad I wanted to be. Not to you and certainly not to Alex."

This caught Veronica completely by surprise. Before she could come up with some kind of response, her father continued, "But all that's going to change. You're going to be seeing a lot more of me . . . and Sandy. What do you have to say about that, Veronica?"

Deflated, Veronica chose her words carefully. "I always want to see more of you."

When she arrived home the next afternoon, Veronica was sorry to see that for once her mother had gotten there early.

"So how was the trip?" Mrs. Volner asked before Veronica had a chance to hang up her jacket.

"Okay."

"Just okay?" Mrs. Volner probed.

"I spent a lot of time falling down."

Veronica's progress on the slopes wasn't what interested Mrs. Volner, though. "So now that you've spent a couple of days with Sandy, what do you think of her?"

"She's okay."

"Will you stop saying everything is okay?" Mrs. Volner asked impatiently.

Veronica grabbed her duffel bag and headed toward her bedroom, with her mother right behind her. "What do you want me to say?"

"Never mind." Her mother turned away.

"She's all over Daddy." Veronica's words stopped Mrs. Volner. "They're always laughing and whispering together. They hardly paid any attention to me."

"They ignored you?" Mrs. Volner frowned.

"Not exactly. I mean, they didn't let me run wild or anything, but they were just so . . . so together."

"Oh."

Veronica felt terrible. Her mother had asked, demanded really, to know what went on, and now that Veronica had told her, she was standing there looking as if she might cry.

"Oh, Mom, Daddy's girlfriends never last very long."

"I know."

"Sandy probably won't be around in a month or so, either."

Mrs. Volner tried to smile. "You're probably right."

But Veronica didn't think she was right, and she knew her mother didn't, either.

C H A P T E R

THREE

"How old was he?" Candy asked, her eyes wide.

Veronica shrugged. "Fifteen. Sixteen, maybe."

"And he just asked if you wanted to play pinball with him?" Lisa crumpled up her lunch bag.

"Yep. He kind of picked me out of the crowd."

"Weren't you nervous?" Kim Chapman inquired. Her best friend, Natalie Wolk, chimed in, "I would have been." Kim and Natalie looked amazingly alike. They both had sparkling brown eyes and straight dark hair that hung to their chins.

Veronica considered her answer to this. She didn't want to say she hadn't been nervous. No one would believe that. On the other hand, acting cool was important. She finally compromised. "A little. After all, he *was* fifteen or sixteen."

Jessica Moriarity leaned forward, a dreamy look on her face. "Then what happened?"

"I had to go back to my room," Veronica said regretfully. Whenever possible, she tried not to lie. She was a master at stretching the truth, though, or bending it so she ended up looking fine. As the girls stared at her, half-envious, half-awed, Veronica knew that she had succeeded in adding even more luster to her image.

Lisa fiddled with her wheat-colored French braid. "Did you see him again?"

"We left the next morning."

"Too bad you didn't meet earlier," Candy said, mooning.

"*C'est la vie,*" Veronica responded with a shrug.

Kim and Natalie looked at each other. "What does that mean?" Kim asked.

"Such is life. French." Veronica's tone implied that anyone who didn't know what the phrase meant was a peasant.

"*C'est la vie,*" Candy mumbled under her breath, as though she was memorizing it.

"So did anything exciting happen to the rest of you?" Veronica asked, but her eyes wandered around the Kennedy Middle School lunchroom. She acted as if she suspected their answers, even Jessica's description of her cruise, would not measure up.

Candy had started in on an anecdote about her grandmother's cats when the bell rang, signaling the lunch hour was over. Saved by the bell, Veronica thought. She led the way out of the lunchroom, moving with the herd of students, and bumped into Billy Page. "Hi, Billy." She twinkled up at him.

"Oh hi, Veronica. I got your card."

"It was quite a trip."

"Yeah. Sounded like it."

Before Veronica could elaborate, Billy said, "Well, I gotta go. You know how Jacobs is if you come in late." Billy, like Jessica and Natalie, was in the other sixth-grade class at Kennedy Middle School. Veronica's teacher was Mrs. Volini, and she didn't like her students to be tardy, either. Veronica would have been willing to chance it, however, if it meant spending a little time talking to Billy. Still, off he loped, leaving her standing in the middle of the hallway.

"What did Billy say?" Candy asked, coming up behind her.

"Oh, we were just talking about my ski trip."

"Was he jealous?"

"Of what?"

"The boy you played pinball with."

"I didn't get to tell him about that," Veronica said. "But I will." At least I hope I will, she thought to herself.

Veronica slid into her seat just as the bell was ringing. Mrs. Volini stood behind her desk waiting for the room to get quiet. Finally, she clapped her hands together to get the class's attention.

"All right, settle down everyone. I know it's hard to get back in the groove after vacation, but let's make the effort, shall we?"

Mrs. Volini's nickname was Mt. Volini. She could really blow her stack when she got angry, and by this point in the year, her students could tell when the lava was starting to boil. Nobody wanted that, so a hush fell over the room.

"All right," she said, pushing some loose hairs back into her bun. "I want to talk about

Career Day. If you remember,"—Mrs. Volini peered at them as if she was sure they didn't— "before vacation I told you that next month the school would be having guest speakers come and talk about their jobs."

Veronica stared out the window. Kennedy Middle School had had Career Days before. Last year, she had been sick on the day when students could sign up to hear the speakers of their choice, and she had been stuck listening to a fireman and an insurance agent.

"Before Career Day arrives, I've decided I'd like to give you a project assignment."

There were a few groans from around the room. Mrs. Volini was famous for her projects. They were always long and involved, and the despised oral report was usually a part of it. Sure enough, Mrs. Volini continued by saying, "I think it would be fun for groups of you to research various occupations and then give oral reports on them."

Now the groans were in unison. There was nothing worse than standing up in front of the class trying to make a topic like "The Legal Profession" interesting to your friends, all of whom wished you would just hurry up and sit down.

Mrs. Volini began boiling. "Well, I'm certainly surprised at this response. We've done other oral reports this year, and I would have hoped by now you would understand how beneficial they are. Not only do they help with your research skills, they allow you to develop your poise in front of a group. . . ."

Idly, Veronica began scribbling Billy's name very lightly on the edge of her notebook. Then she turned her pencil over and erased what she had written. Billy hadn't been very nice to her in the hallway. She wondered why.

"Now, if any of you have a special affiliation with someone in a certain profession, let me know. For instance, one interesting field might be the arts. Does anyone know an artist or a writer?"

Everyone turned and looked at Bobby Glickman. He was a professional actor. He had been in several local plays and television commercials, anyway.

Short, and a little shy unless he was on camera, Bobby shrugged. "I know someone who wrote a play I was in."

"Excellent." Mrs. Volini beamed. "Anyone else?"

Veronica was pulled out of her daydream

when she heard her own name mentioned. "Veronica knows a writer," Candy was saying proudly.

Veronica turned and gave her a horrified look.

"Is that true, Veronica? You could interview someone about writing?"

She desperately wanted to say no, but that would take too much explanation. "Yes."

"Fine. Then we'll put you down to work with Bobby. And didn't you have your hand raised, Gretchen?"

Gretchen's hands were now folded tightly in a ball.

"Gretchen?"

"My mother's a writer, and she teaches it, too," Gretchen finally said, her voice low.

"Very good. Well, we have our first group: Bobby, Veronica, and Gretchen. And I'm expecting an extra-good report since you have so many sources on which to draw. Now, who knows someone in the medical profession?"

Veronica didn't know whether to be more angry at Candy, for suggesting she interview Sandy, or Gretchen, for having a mother who taught writing. Sandy and Gretchen involved in one project—she never would have believed it was possible.

She was still mad when the last bell rang. Brushing off Candy, Veronica strode to her locker and started pulling out books to take home.

"Hey, what's wrong?" a bewildered Candy asked, walking over to her.

Veronica opened her mouth to tell Candy, then realized she couldn't confess that she didn't like Sandy. "I don't feel like working with hippos, okay? I thought a human partner might be nice."

"Bobby will be on the committee, too."

"Oh, he's stuck-up," she muttered, even though that wasn't true. Then, looking at Candy thoughtfully, Veronica said, "What did you wind up with?"

Candy wrinkled her nose. "Salespeople."

"Salespeople." Veronica smiled. "Great."

Before Candy could say anything, Veronica tugged on her hand and pulled her across the aisle, where Gretchen was slipping on her coat.

"I need to talk to you," Veronica said authoritatively. Veronica felt comfortable bossing almost everyone, but Gretchen was a special case. Veronica could intimidate Gretchen just by raising her eyebrow. Maybe it was because Gretchen was overweight or because she had been a loner, at least until Robin had lifted her out of obscurity. Gretchen always looked so hopeful when Veronica was around—like a puppy dog just waiting to be fed a scrap from the table.

Gretchen fumbled in her pocket for her hat. "What about?" she asked, not looking directly at Veronica.

"Our project." She put an ironic emphasis on the word *our*.

"When do you want to get together?"

"I don't."

Now Gretchen faced Veronica. "We're supposed to do it together."

"I want you to trade with Candy."

Candy looked at Veronica with surprise. "You do?"

Veronica said sweetly, "Candy has a perfectly good topic—salespeople. You could interview a clerk at the grocery store or anybody." She turned to Candy. "And your brother writes for the high school newspaper, right?"

"Yes, but he's not a real writer. . . ."

Veronica frowned. "Sure he is. Real enough for Career Day. So why don't the two of you just tell Mrs. Volini you want to switch."

Gretchen looked nervous. Candy didn't

seem much happier, but she shrugged and said, "I guess I could."

"But I don't want to," Gretchen said in a barely audible voice.

Veronica let out an exaggerated sigh. "Gretchen, don't you get it? I don't want to work with you."

Now a stubborn expression settled on Gretchen's face. "Then ask Mrs. Volini for another assignment."

Veronica was shocked. Gretchen had never talked back to her before. She always had been so eager to be one of the in crowd, she usually did whatever Veronica asked. Veronica didn't know what to say. Gretchen shrugged, threw her backpack over her shoulder, and left Candy and Veronica alone in the hallway.

"Boy, what got into her?" Candy asked.

"I don't know," Veronica said through tight lips. "She's going to be sorry she didn't trade, though."

"What are you going to do to her?" Candy demanded eagerly.

"I don't know. But I think I will ask Mrs. Volini to be on another committee." Any profession that didn't involve writers would do.

She hurried back into the room, but when she sweetly told Mrs. Volini she wanted to change, the teacher shook her head. "It's too late, Veronica. Everyone's been assigned." She peered at Veronica. "What's the problem?"

It was too embarrassing to explain. "Nothing, really," she mumbled.

"Well, then . . ."

Defeated, Veronica went outside to catch her bus. She often got a ride with her mother in the morning, but she had to take the bus home in the afternoon. She usually sat with Candy, but Candy had to go to the dentist today. The bus was almost full, and there were only two single seats left. One of them was next to Robin Miller. Veronica hesitated, then she sat down. She wasn't about to let Robin think she was afraid to share a bus seat with her.

Robin averted her head, but then she turned to Veronica and said, "Hello, Veronica."

"Hi."

The silence lengthened, and Robin reached into her backpack and took out a paperback book. Before she could begin reading it, Veronica asked, "How was your vacation?"

Robin looked at her with surprise. It had been a long time since they had had a normal conversation. Veronica wasn't quite sure why she was starting one now, but it seemed like a good thing to do.

"It was all right," Robin began slowly. "We didn't do much. My cousins came for a visit."

"I went on a ski trip with my father and his girlfriend."

"Which one?" When Robin and Veronica had been best friends, they had had lots of conversations about Mr. Volner and the women he dated.

"A new one—Sandy."

"Do you like her?"

"No," Veronica answered shortly. With a start, she realized Robin was the only one she had shared the truth with.

Robin shrugged. "Well, she'll probably be gone soon."

This time, Veronica was honest. "I don't think so. Not this one."

"Really?" Robin asked with surprise.

Veronica, suddenly scared, didn't feel like confiding any further in Robin. There was no guarantee that Robin wouldn't go spilling her secrets to everyone, even though she never had done anything like that in the past. Instead, Veronica said, "Say, I see Gretchen is a real pal of yours now."

Robin stiffened. "So what if she is?"

"I'm going to be working on that stupid Career Day project with her."

"I know," Robin replied bluntly. "I was there, remember?"

"Oh yeah. You're working with Jonathan, aren't you? That's a coincidence," she added sarcastically. She was pleased to see she still could make Robin blush.

"My father's a teacher and his mother is studying to be one. It's no big deal."

"But that will be so much fun—you and Jonathan getting to discuss how teachers make out lesson plans."

"I forgot how funny you could be." Robin picked up her book.

Veronica had an idea, though. "You know, I don't think Gretchen is going to enjoy working with me," she said, more sweetly.

"Probably not."

"Then why should she do it? Candy said she'd trade with her."

Robin shook her head, her red curls quivering. "I don't want any part of this, Veronica."

"It just doesn't make sense for both of us to be miserable."

"If Gretchen wants to trade, she will." With

that, Robin opened her book and started reading.

To Veronica's surprise, Robin's dismissal of her didn't make her angry. She felt sad. For a few minutes, it seemed as if she and Robin might be embarking on a normal conversation.

So what? Veronica thought to herself. Making a big show of it, she pulled a book out of her own backpack. She barely noticed which one it was. The uncomfortable silence continued until it was time for Robin to get off the bus.

As Robin pushed past her, she muttered, "Bye."

"Bye," Veronica responded involuntarily. She watched Robin walk down the aisle and through the open bus doors.

The next day, during social studies, Mrs. Volini went into more detail about what she expected from the oral reports. "As I stressed earlier in the year, I want lively, upbeat reports."

In the back row, Ham Berger stuck his finger down his throat and discreetly mimed throwing up. Veronica thought Ham was an obnoxious boor, but in this case she had to agree with him.

"Each of you, of course, will interview someone in the field you've chosen. Ask your people what they like and dislike about their jobs. What training did they have and how did they first get into their professions? Are they planning to continue with them? Well, you're smart children. I'm sure you can come up with all sorts of interesting questions. Along with your individual interviews, there are also things I'd like you to work on as a committee. You will be graded individually and as a group. Find out the history of your professions. How do women and minorities fare in them? Who are some famous people involved in these areas? You can make charts or graphs; anything visual would be lovely." She lowered her voice conspiratorially. "Perhaps if we're very lucky, some of our charts will be used to help spruce up the gym on Career Day."

Career Day was always held in the gym. Smelling of old sweat and needing a coat of paint, the gym, in Veronica's opinion, would not be noticeably spruced up by a few sixth-grade posters.

"I'm going to give you a few moments now for your committees to meet, so you can discuss how you are going to arrange for your interviews and organize your reports."

There was a general shuffle as the groups of twos and threes got together. Veronica stayed firmly planted in her seat. Bobby and Gretchen knew where to find her.

She almost laughed as they approached. Talk about Jack Sprat and his fat wife—Bobby was wiry, his thin arms sticking out of his T-shirt. Gretchen walked slowly behind him.

If Gretchen was on a diet, it hadn't helped much yet. Maybe her round face was a little thinner, but her tummy still wiggled like Jell-O. Thick blond hair hung around the sides of her face in no particular style, and her pale blue eyes refused to focus on Veronica, even though she was right in front of her.

"So," Veronica began when they had come close enough, "what are we going to do about this stupid report?"

Bobby shrugged. "It won't be that bad. I'll talk to this playwright, and Gretchen can talk to her mother, and you . . . who's your writer?"

"She works on a magazine," Veronica replied curtly.

"Okay. We can start out by explaining what it takes to be a writer and then talk about real famous ones, like Shakespeare."

"Yes, Shakespeare would be good, Bobby,"

Veronica said dryly. "What about the history of writing? And we can have some sort of a chart about the different ways to get things into print, like the first printing presses and then typewriters and computers."

"Not bad," Bobby said approvingly.

"We can talk about how hard it is to be a writer," Gretchen said, so quietly that they could barely hear her. "My mother has to teach as well as write, because it's hard to support herself as a writer."

"Yeah, that's good, too." Bobby flashed her a smile. "We've got lots of good ideas, huh?"

"Most of them were mine," Veronica said.

Bobby ignored that. "We should get together, I guess, and figure out who is going to do what. We can't meet at my house, though. My brother's just getting over the chicken pox."

When Veronica didn't say anything, Gretchen finally offered, "You can come to my house Sunday?" she asked.

"Okay by me," Bobby replied. He looked at Veronica, who shrugged her acceptance. "Well, I guess we're done." Without a backward glance, he wandered over to talk to Ham Berger, who apparently had exhausted his ideas about his career topic—insurance agents—and was back at his desk, eating a bag of M&Ms.

Veronica glanced at Gretchen's outfit, a loose overblouse and jeans. Gretchen was not noted for fashion sense.

"What are you going to wear when you give your oral report, Gretchen?"

Gretchen looked bewildered. "I don't know."

"Maybe you could find something nice in the maternity department. I'm sure they have lots of wonderful, roomy outfits there."

Veronica watched Gretchen's face redden. It was a nice, apple-y shade of red, and Veronica felt very good knowing that she had caused it.

C H A P T E R
FOUR

Veronica rummaged through her closet. She pulled out a red velvet dress and then hung it back up—too babyish. Quickly, she discarded her new pants as too informal and a plaid skirt with a matching maroon sweater as boring. It had been a long time since she had gone out with her father for a meal alone, and Veronica wanted to be dressed just right. Unfortunately, the right outfit didn't seem to be in her closet at the moment.

"Mom," Veronica screamed downstairs.

"What is it?" Mrs. Volner called from the kitchen, where she was reading the Sunday newspaper over a second cup of coffee.

"Could you come up here?"

There was a silence, and then Mrs. Volner responded, "Must I?"

"I want to ask you something."

Veronica could hear her mother muttering something as she scraped her chair away from the kitchen table and headed upstairs.

"What is it?" she asked when she got to the doorway of Veronica's room.

Even on a Sunday, Mrs. Volner looked dressed up. Today, she wore a soft, fuzzy pink sweater and black wool pants. She should be able to help pick out the perfect thing.

"I don't have anything to wear when Daddy and I go out."

"Veronica, you have a closetful of clothes."

"I hate them all."

Mrs. Volner shook her head, but instead of arguing with Veronica, she just headed over to the closet and started looking through it. "Do you know where your father is taking you?"

"The Palace," she said, naming a nearby restaurant where they had a lavish Sunday brunch.

"We used to go there," Mrs. Volner murmured as she pulled out a navy dress with a lace collar. "What about this?"

Veronica took the dress without really looking at it. "You and Daddy used to go to the Palace?"

Mrs. Volner looked distracted. "Yes, but usually on Saturday night."

"Mom?"

"What?"

There was a question Veronica had wanted to ask for a long time, and for once, the moment seemed right to voice it. "Do you miss Daddy?"

Mrs. Volner started to say something, then shook her head. "No, not anymore."

A chilly loneliness spread through Veronica. So she was the only one who missed her father. It embarrassed her to think that she wasn't able to distance herself from her father the way that everyone else in her family had.

"Is that dress all right?" her mother asked.

Veronica glanced at it. Suddenly, what she wore didn't seem that important anymore. "It's fine."

By the time Veronica had fixed her hair into a long braid, her father's car was in the driveway. He never came inside the house.

"Have a good time," Mrs. Volner called in a dull voice from the kitchen.

Veronica slipped out the door and hurried

to the car. To her dismay, Sandy was sitting next to her father.

"Hello, Veronica," Sandy said gaily as Veronica got into the backseat. "I hope you don't mind me joining you."

Veronica didn't say anything. She wasn't going to lie.

"How are you, sweetie?" her father asked.

"Fine." Veronica's tone was clipped.

"Good. That's good. Say, how about a change of plans?" He sounded a little nervous.

"What do you mean?"

"Well, there's an antiques show at the University Exposition Hall that Sandy wants to go to. We can probably grab something to eat there, and then you girls will have a chance to shop, too."

"Antiques?" Veronica wrinkled her nose.

"Your father told me you like to look at collectibles. But we don't have to go."

"It's all right," Veronica said with a sigh. She figured she could get a lot of mileage out of accepting the change in plans.

On the way to the Exposition Hall, Mr. Volner chatted about all sorts of silly things, like the chances for the Chicago Bears to get into the Super Bowl. Sandy added her own inane comments about how she was turning into a football expert. Veronica stared out the window at the passing landscape.

By the time they pulled into the parking lot, Veronica had made it clear, without saying a word, that she was unhappy. Mr. Volner dealt with this by talking a little louder and a little faster. Sandy, though, fell into the same bleak silence that Veronica was perfecting.

Fortunately, talking was difficult anyway as they made their way down the crowded aisles of the antiques show, and the lack of communication didn't seem quite so obvious. Sandy was right; Veronica usually did like looking at old pieces. But as she moved past table after table filled with china, pottery, glassware, and jewelry, everything began to look the same.

Sandy seemed particularly interested in the jewelry. "Oh look, Neal," she said, admiring a pearl ring surrounded by diamonds that she had put on her ring finger.

"Do you like it?"

"Yes." She looked at it critically. "I think so."

As Sandy wavered over her decision, Veronica wandered over to a small stall where a salt and pepper shaker set in the shape of two pigs sat on a bookshelf. They looked so familiar. Then Veronica remembered that the Volners used to have a set like that when she was small. "Daddy," she called, "come look."

Mr. Volner said something to Sandy and walked over to Veronica. "Remember these?" she asked, pointing to the salt and pepper shakers.

Mr. Volner's smile was wistful. "Uncle Jerry gave your mother and me a set like that as a wedding gift . . . kind of a joke. You used to play with them."

"What happened to them?"

"I took them with me when I moved out. One of them broke, so I threw the other one away."

Veronica picked up the pepper shaker. She remembered how she had always acted out "The Three Little Pigs" with them, even though there were only two.

"Would you like them?" her father asked.

Seeing the eager look on Mr. Volner's face, she put them down with a thud. "No."

"Are you sure?"

Veronica tried to make her tone scornful. "What would I do with salt and pepper shakers?" Her eyes strayed to the booth where Sandy was still trying on different rings. "I'm hungry."

"There's a small café over there." He pointed to tables set up in a corner of the vast hall.

"It's not the Palace," Veronica said under her breath, but she headed for them anyway.

Once they were settled with chicken-salad sandwiches, Sandy tried once more to get the conversation going. Veronica just watched the passing crowds. Mr. Volner and Sandy exchanged glances; then, in a casual tone, Sandy asked, "How's school, Veronica?"

"Fine."

"Learning anything interesting?"

Veronica looked at her with the disdain she felt Sandy's stupid question deserved. "Yes. Christopher Columbus discovered America. Have you heard?" It was a babyish answer, but it evoked the response that Veronica wanted. Sandy lowered her eyes and began nibbling on her sandwich.

Mr. Volner's eyes narrowed. "That was unnecessary."

Veronica pushed away her food. "I thought we were going to have lunch alone," she said, finally voicing the thought that had been stuck in her throat all afternoon.

"We are alone, the three of us."

"Do we have to stay here much longer?" she asked.

Mr. Volner sighed. "I guess not. Sandy and I were going to tell you something today, but obviously the time's not right."

Veronica was immediately alert. "What was it?"

Sandy shook her head slightly, piquing Veronica's interest even more.

"No. You're not in the proper frame of mind." Mr. Volner adopted Veronica's sarcastic tone.

Torn between wanting to know what was going on and keeping her aloofness intact, Veronica decided to say nothing. If they weren't going to tell her, she wasn't going to beg. Mr. Volner and Sandy began talking about their jobs, leaving Veronica to finish her sandwich. She knew that she should ask Sandy about setting up an interview for her Career Day project, but she wasn't in the proper frame of mind for that, either. She didn't think she'd ever be.

When her father took her out in the middle of the day, he would usually ask whether Veronica wanted to go to a movie with him. Today, Mr. Volner and Sandy just dropped her off at home. He didn't even kiss her good-bye.

Veronica let herself into an empty house. Her mother had told her earlier she was going shopping at the mall with friends. Flinging off the now-hated navy dress, Veronica was about to throw it in the closet when the phone rang. "Hello?" she answered in a sharp tone.

"Veronica, it's Bobby."

"What is it?" Veronica wasn't in the mood to be nice to him, either.

"I'm at Gretchen's. You're supposed to be here, too," he said bluntly. "Remember?"

Now she did. "I just got home from lunch with my father. I'll be there as soon as I can." She hung up without saying good-bye.

As she put on a sweatshirt and jeans, Veronica wondered whether there was anything she wanted to do less than go to Gretchen's. Spending more time with her father and Sandy was the only thing that came to mind. After writing a note to her mother, Veronica headed out into the snow-laced air.

Veronica knew where Gretchen lived; it wasn't very far. Gretchen's father opened the door. She didn't know what she expected Mr. Hubbard to look like—probably some overweight dolt like Gretchen. A perfectly decent-looking man wearing a plaid shirt and jeans stood in front of her.

"Hello, Veronica, I've heard a lot about you."

Veronica had the good grace to be embarrassed. She could imagine what Gretchen must have told him. "Hi," she mumbled.

He pointed the way to the kitchen, and Veronica could feel him staring at her back.

Bobby and Gretchen were sitting at the kitchen table, various papers spread out in front of them.

Veronica looked around curiously as she settled herself in the kitchen. She hadn't expected to like Gretchen's house, either, but there was a cheeriness to the room that Veronica couldn't help but respond to. Perky white eyelet curtains adorned the windows and the delicious smell of cookies baking emanated from the oven.

"Oh, hi," Bobby said. Gretchen was silent.

"So what have you done so far?" Veronica asked, taking a seat across from them.

"We're doing the introduction. The good and bad sides of being a writer." He patted a small stack of library books. "These help, but we really should do our interviews and get those opinions in."

Veronica looked over the books. Bobby hadn't been able to find anything very helpful about William Shakespeare, but he had taken out biographies of Carl Sandburg and Mark Twain that were written for kids. There were two books about the history of writing and a picture book about how books were made. She was pleased that Bobby had done so much work. That meant less for her.

"Have you set up your interview yet?" he continued.

Sandy's face passed in front of her. "No, not yet."

"I did. And Gretchen's going to call her mother tonight."

"Call her?" Veronica looked at Gretchen curiously.

"My mother lives in New Mexico." Gretchen offered nothing more.

"Your parents are divorced?"

"No," Gretchen said emphatically. "My mother just wanted to try living there for a while."

"She teaches writing at the university," Bobby said.

Veronica pulled one of the books over and flipped through the pages. When her father had moved out, he'd said he just wanted to try living apart for a while. Veronica wondered whether she should tell Gretchen that she'd better not count on her parents getting back together.

Bobby didn't seem to notice the tension that crackled in the air. "What about you? You're interviewing someone who works on a magazine, right?"

"I'll get to it."

"Soon, Veronica. Like I said, we should put some of the interview stuff in the introduction."

"I said I'd do it," Veronica replied irritably.

Gretchen got up. "I'll take the cookies out."

"You made them? From scratch?" Veronica asked with surprise as Gretchen expertly got them out of the oven and put them on a plate.

"Sure, why not?"

"You're right. Anyone who likes to eat as much as . . ." Veronica's voice trailed off as she noticed the frown on Bobby's face. It was different making fun of Gretchen in front of a boy. Veronica wasn't quite sure why.

They worked for a half hour dividing up the topics. Along with her interview, Veronica was going to discuss famous writers. She agreed to read the biographies of Carl Sandburg and Mark Twain, but she thought she might like to include a writer the kids actually would have read, like Judy Blume.

"We've got it all straight then," Bobby said, authoritatively making notes. "Veronica, famous writers; Gretchen, the different kinds of writing; and I'll do how technology has changed writing."

Veronica scowled. "Who made you chairman of this project?"

Bobby looked up in surprise. "Do you want to do it?"

She didn't, but fortunately, a horn blew outside and Bobby got up before Veronica could respond. "That's my mom. We're going over to my cousin's house."

Veronica would have liked a ride home, but she didn't want to inconvenience the Glickmans if it was out of their way. She supposed she could walk back.

After Bobby hurried out, Veronica put on her own jacket, which she had flung over a kitchen chair. She took another cookie. They were good. "Hey, you didn't eat any of these."

"No, I didn't."

Realization dawned. "Because of your diet!"

Gretchen just shrugged.

The words *it's about time* almost slipped from Veronica's lips, but even with Bobby gone, something stopped her. Maybe it was the expression on Gretchen's face, a mixture of embarrassment and hope.

Mr. Hubbard stuck his head into the kitchen. "Gretchen, don't forget to call your mom. You don't want to miss her."

"No, I'll do it as soon as Veronica leaves."

"I'm leaving now."

Gretchen walked Veronica to the front door.

"It's not going to get easier, you know."

"What?"

"When your parents get divorced. It's only going to be more complicated. Take it from me; I know." Veronica felt the least she could do was enlighten Gretchen.

"They might not get divorced," Gretchen said stiffly. "My father says they haven't even talked about it."

Veronica shrugged. "Parents say that. They do whatever they want anyway."

A stubborn look crossed Gretchen's face. "Well, that was your family. This is just temporary."

Veronica found herself feeling a little sorry for Gretchen. Even though she had been much younger, she could clearly remember having a similar argument with Alex. She kept telling him that their parents might get back together, and he had told her over and over again to forget it. Veronica wished now that she had listened to him. It might have saved her a lot of hoping. Opening the door, she decided to say only, "Just don't be disappointed if things don't work out the way you want."

As Veronica walked home, she stuffed mittened hands into her pockets for extra warmth. She felt confused. Why was she beginning to feel sorry for Gretchen? She was such a nerd. Yet Veronica couldn't deny the small bubble of sympathy that was floating around inside her. It wasn't an emotion she felt very often, but she knew that when your parents were having problems, it was no time to start adding more. If anyone knew that, it was she.

C H A P T E R

FIVE

Veronica watched from the end of the hallway as Billy opened his locker and took out his gym bag.

As she fiddled with her own backpack, Veronica caught Billy's eyes on her. Would he come over? Should she go over there? Veronica wasn't sure who should make the next move.

Maybe she could just walk past him. After all, he stood between her and the door. Tossing her hair over her shoulder, she followed a string of kids who were leaving the building.

"Hi, Veronica," Billy said, his voice stopping her.

"Oh, hi." She gave him a smile. "Big game tonight, huh?"

"Yeah. The Wilmot Hornets."

"But you're going to win, aren't you?"

Billy frowned. "I hope so. I wish Rossi hadn't quit the team, though. What a jerk."

"Why did he quit?" Veronica asked curiously. The basketball team, except as it affected Billy as the star, wasn't of much interest to her. But she had liked Jonathan at one time, and she wondered why he had dropped out.

"He just didn't want to play anymore." Billy laughed harshly. "Can you believe it? Just when he started playing halfway decently, too. He could have helped the Wildcats, but he didn't feel like it."

Actually, Veronica could sympathize. She never wanted to bother with things she didn't feel like doing, either. However, voicing her support for Jonathan didn't seem like a good idea with Billy scowling down at her.

"I wonder if there's going to be another dance at the community center."

Billy looked a little fuzzy.

"Like the holiday dance. Maybe something for Valentine's Day."

"Oh yeah. Well, maybe." He went back to stuffing a notebook in his gym bag.

This wasn't going the way Veronica had hoped. By now, Billy should be talking about going to The Hut for ice cream, not messing around with some smelly gym socks. She stood there uncertainly for a minute; then, in what she hoped was a casual voice, she said, "See you at the game."

"Sure."

There was nothing left for Veronica to do but leave.

Candy was waiting outside the school door. "I thought we were supposed to meet here," she said with a pout.

"I was talking to Billy."

Candy now nodded understandingly. On Veronica's scale, Candy knew that she fell several notches below Billy. "You're going to the game tonight, aren't you? My mother can drive us."

"I guess," Veronica said listlessly.

"What's with you? You wouldn't miss a chance to see Billy play."

Veronica pasted a smile on her face. "No, of course not. I just have a headache, that's all." She rubbed her forehead in what she hoped was a convincing manner.

Immediately concerned, Candy said, "Should we go and get some aspirin?"

"Oh, that's all right," Veronica said, "I'll be okay."

Lisa came up to make arrangements for joining them at the game. By the time they piled into the Dahls' van that evening, Jessica had decided to go along, too.

"I hope the Wildcats win tonight," Jessica said, pushing Lisa over so that she had a little more room in the backseat.

"Me, too. It's so gruesome when they lose," Candy added.

Lisa threw Jessica a sly look. "Veronica doesn't care how it comes out as long as Billy has a good game."

Veronica's smile was noncommittal.

"Veronica and Billy were talking this afternoon," Candy informed the girls importantly.

"Ooh, what did he say?" Lisa demanded.

"He just talked about the game," Veronica replied. Changing the subject, she said, "Do you think I should have boys at my birthday party?" Veronica's twelfth birthday was coming up soon.

"Yes," Lisa and Jessica said in unison.

Mrs. Dahl looked at Veronica in the rearview mirror. "You just had a boy-girl party at Halloween, Veronica. And there was the dance just a few weeks ago. Don't you think you girls are pushing this sort of thing?"

Candy looked mortified. "Moth-er," she said, drawing out the syllables.

"You're only in sixth grade," Mrs. Dahl said mildly.

"Well, I haven't decided about the party yet," Veronica said politely.

"Have you discussed this with your mom?"

"Not yet."

There was an embarrassed silence in the car. Candy rolled her eyes as if to say, What can you expect? Fortunately, the school was in sight, so Candy was spared any more humiliation.

The girls thanked Mrs. Dahl for the ride as they climbed out of the car. "I'll meet you here after the game," she said.

It was fun to be at the brightly lit school at night. The Wildcats drew a pretty good crowd, despite the ups and downs they had had during the season. The girls pushed into the gym and found seats in the middle of the bleachers.

"Look at that guy on the Hornets," Lisa said, pointing to a tall boy bouncing a basketball.

"Cute," Jessica said approvingly.

Veronica's eyes wandered over to the other side of the court, where Billy stood talking to Coach Davidson. She willed Billy to look at her, but he continued his conversation, oblivious.

"There're Gretchen and Robin and Sharon," Candy whispered in her ear.

Veronica gave the threesome, a few seats away, a cursory glance.

"How has it been, working on that report with her?" Candy asked.

Veronica didn't like remembering feeling sorry for Gretchen. "About what you'd expect. It's a big pain," she added, emphasizing the word *big*.

"You know, I think she's losing weight," Jessica said, looking over at Gretchen critically.

"Yeah, she told me she's on a diet."

"It won't help." Lisa giggled. "She'll still have that dirty-blonde hair."

"And those clothes," Candy added, wrinkling her nose. "My grandmother dresses better than she does."

"Well, we all know how fashionable your grandmother is." Lisa laughed. "She's the earring queen, right?"

"Funny," Candy muttered.

Veronica banished whatever sympathy she might have felt for Gretchen. "Maybe I ought to lend my fellow committee member something to wear when she gives her oral report," she said sarcastically.

"Like she'd fit into anything of yours." Jessica hooted.

"Sew two of your skirts together," Candy said. "That might work."

"But it would take more than two of your blouses." Lisa choked back her laughter. "Have you noticed how busty she's getting?"

At the word *busty*, the girls got hysterical.

"Gretchen Hubbard, future *Playboy* Playmate." Veronica snorted.

"Oh yuk." Lisa made a face, then stuck out her chest. "Here I am, boys."

The girls broke off into gales of laughter. Gretchen turned at the sound of their giggles. When Candy and Lisa noticed her looking at them, they laughed even harder.

Gretchen shifted toward Robin, and Veronica could see her nervously clasping and unclasping her hands. Veronica felt a flash of guilt, but it quickly passed. Gretchen was still blubbery, and busty, too, for that matter. Why should she feel bad about laughing at her? Everything that had been said was the truth.

The referee's whistle drew everyone's attention to the court. The game got off to an exciting start, first with the Wildcats making a basket, then the Hornets, but Veronica's attention wandered. Basketball players always seemed to her like a pack of dogs running up and down the court. Unless Billy had the ball in his hand, Veronica simply wasn't very interested.

Unaware of the cheers filling the air all around her, Veronica began thinking about her father. He hadn't called since their awful outing. So he's mad, Veronica said to herself. So what? If anyone should be angry, it's me.

She thought back to the first time she had ever seen Sandy. It had been at her father's apartment downtown. Veronica hadn't met too many of her father's girlfriends, even though he mentioned them now and then. That night, Veronica was going to sleep over, and she and her father had rented a videotape to watch. They had just finished their carryout Chinese food when Mr. Volner asked, "Would you mind if someone joined us tonight, Veronica?"

"To watch *Gone With the Wind?*"

Mr. Volner got up and began scraping the dishes. He didn't look at Veronica as he said, "Yes, it's one of Sandy's favorite movies."

"Who's Sandy?" Veronica demanded suspiciously.

"A woman I've been dating."

"I figured that. I meant, is she someone that you've been seeing for a while?"

"No. Actually, I just met her a couple of weeks ago."

This struck Veronica as odd. The one or two girlfriends she had met had been in the picture for a while. Crumpling up her napkin, she said, "I guess I don't care."

"Good!" Mr. Volner was relieved. "I'll just call and tell her it's okay." Veronica noticed the smile on her father's face and the upbeat note in his voice as he told Sandy to hurry up and come over. Seeing her father so excited was gross.

While they were waiting for Sandy to arrive, Mr. Volner put some popcorn in the microwave and chattered about how much fun they were all going to have together. The more he talked, the more worried Veronica became.

Still, when Sandy walked in, it was hard not to be impressed. She was pretty, no doubt about that, and she included Veronica in her warm smile. Veronica could feel herself responding to Sandy's enthusiasm for the movie.

"I always wished I could be Scarlet O'Hara," Sandy said as she took a handful of popcorn.

"The way she could wrap men around her finger," she added with a wink.

Mr. Volner had walked over to her, put his hand lightly on her shoulder, and said, "Scarlet O'Hara had nothing on you."

Alarm bells went off in Veronica's head. Mr. Volner had never acted so drippy around a woman. Usually, he seemed very polite, but distant, as if trying not to offend Veronica. Now, however, he stood in front of her, smiling at Sandy, with a silly grin plastered all over his face.

Veronica had made an effort to be nice that first evening. She'd answered all of Sandy's questions about school and her friends, and even shared a tissue with her during some of the sadder moments of the movie. However, when it became obvious that Sandy wasn't ready to leave when Veronica went off to bed, her mixed feelings about Sandy began to harden into dislike.

Now Sandy and her father were closer than ever. Whatever they had wanted to tell her on Sunday, she was certain it was something she didn't want to hear.

"Hey"—Candy punched her in the arm—"stop daydreaming. Billy just made a basket."

Veronica refocused her eyes on the court and joined in the yells of the crowd. It was pointless to worry about her father and Sandy.

She was forced to think about them again the following Saturday, however. Veronica had planned to do a little shopping with her mother; and afterward, Gretchen and Bobby were coming over to work on their project— not that Veronica had yet done her share of the research. Thinking of the project always reminded her of Sandy, so she had put it off. She would have to fake it this afternoon, or maybe she could ask her mother to stop at the library, so at least she would have a book or two for the sake of appearance.

A trip to the library wasn't much to ask of her mother after Mrs. Volner had fouled up the brilliant plan Veronica had had earlier in the week.

"Mom, you know lots of writers, don't you?" Veronica had asked, going into her mother's bathroom.

Mrs. Volner was taking off her makeup, getting ready for bed. "Yes, there are copywriters at the advertising agency."

"Well, remember that Career Day thing I

told you about? I need to interview a writer for that. Why don't you let me talk to someone at the agency?"

Mrs. Volner stopped wiping off the cold cream from her face. "I thought you were going to interview Sandy."

"I don't want to. I haven't even asked her yet. Interviewing someone from the agency would be perfect."

"I don't think so, Veronica. If you're supposed to talk to Sandy, you should."

"But no one would ever know the difference," Veronica said in a whining voice.

"You shouldn't avoid talking to Sandy. If you interview her, you'll get a chance to know her better."

"Oh, Mom, I don't want to!"

"Stick to the original plan," Mrs. Volner had said, turning back to the mirror.

For once, Veronica hadn't been able to make her mother change her mind.

Yes, she'd have to tell her mother to stop at the library. It was imperative to have a few books so at least it would look as if she had done something. Veronica was just putting on her coat when the phone rang. "I'll get it," her mother said.

Mrs. Volner's end of the conversation was

very odd. "I see," her mother said after a silence. Then: "Well, we did, but I suppose we'll have to change them." Without a good-bye, she hung up.

"Who was that?" Veronica asked, coming into the kitchen.

"Your father."

"Daddy? What did he want?"

Mrs. Volner sat down at the kitchen table and pulled a cigarette out of the pack she had in her sweater pocket. Veronica hated it when her mother smoked, but she knew better than to hassle her about it when she looked so upset. "He wants to talk to us," Mrs. Volner responded, her tone clipped.

Veronica slid into a seat across from her. "About what?"

"I'm not sure, but it's something serious."

Now Veronica was starting to get scared. "He's not sick, is he?"

Mrs. Volner turned to her daughter and saw her concern. "Oh no, honey, I'm sure it's nothing like that." She rubbed Veronica's hand in both of hers.

"You're sure?"

"Yes." Striking a match, Mrs. Volner lit her cigarette and blew some smoke into the air.

Veronica could read her mother well enough

to know when she wasn't telling her the whole truth. "Then what is it? You have some idea about what it could be, don't you?"

Mrs. Volner gazed at her daughter. "I do. I suppose it's your father's place to tell you, but I'm not going to lie. I think it has something to do with him and Sandy."

Veronica felt as if she was falling, and she put her hand against the edge of the table to steady herself. Though she had had these thoughts herself, hearing her mother voice them made them shockingly real. "They're getting married?"

"He didn't say, Veronica. Just that he wants to tell us about a big change in his life."

"Maybe he's going to change jobs," Veronica said desperately.

Mrs. Volner stubbed out the cigarette, even though she had inhaled only a few puffs. "I don't think so."

Tears began to fill Veronica's eyes. She lowered her head so her mother wouldn't see her cry. "I don't want him to get remarried, especially not to Sandy."

Wearily, Mrs. Volner said, "We don't always get the things we'd like in life, Veronica. I can tell you all about that."

Veronica looked up with surprise. "You told me you didn't love Daddy anymore."

"I don't. But your father was an important part of my life. I'm not sure I like the idea of his being married to someone else, either."

"Maybe there's something we could say . . . or do."

Mrs. Volner shook her head. "That's silly, Veronica."

"I'm not silly." Now her tears started to fall in earnest.

Her mother took a napkin from the plastic holder on the kitchen table and handed it to Veronica. "I just meant that sometimes you have to accept things whether you like them or not. You'll make it harder on yourself if you don't."

Veronica understood what her mother was trying to tell her, but that didn't mean she had to believe it. Determination began flowing through her. When her father arrived, she was going to tell him just what she thought about his plans.

"How about some hot chocolate?" Mrs. Volner said with a sigh.

Hot chocolate was the last thing Veronica wanted, but her mother looked so helpless toying with her cigarette butt that Veronica nodded a mute assent.

Mrs. Volner pushed herself away from the kitchen table and put water into the teakettle. While she searched the cabinet above the sink for the hot-chocolate mix, Veronica began thinking of what her father's remarriage would mean to her.

From what she had already seen of her father and Sandy's relationship, she knew that it would exclude her. Oh, she supposed they both had good intentions about making her feel a part of things, but how could they? They certainly hadn't up until now.

Then another thought struck her. There would be another Mrs. Volner. Even though her parents had been divorced for a while, that name belonged to her mother. It made Veronica a little sick to think now she would be sharing it with Sandy.

Her mother squirted some whipped cream into the steaming mug of chocolate. "I wonder if they're planning on having children," she murmured.

"What?" Veronica snapped to attention. That horrible thought hadn't entered her mind.

Noticing Veronica's shock, Mrs. Volner

said, "Sorry, darling, I shouldn't have mentioned that. I was just thinking out loud." She placed the hot chocolate in front of Veronica. The sweet smell coming from the cup didn't help the unsettled feeling in her stomach.

"He wouldn't."

"Sandy's very young. She probably wants children of her own."

"But Daddy already has children," Veronica said, trying to gain control of her emotions.

Mrs. Volner didn't say anything, but the pitying look on her face spoke volumes.

Veronica took an unwanted sip of her drink. She wanted nothing so much as to go up to her room, climb into bed, and put the covers over her head. Instead, the doorbell rang, and Veronica got up to answer it.

Her father stood on the front steps, looking very jaunty in a parka and jeans. "Hi, sweetie," he said. "It's cold out here; let me in, please." Without waiting for an answer, he entered the house.

Mrs. Volner came out into the hall. "Neal, let me take your coat." As he slipped it off, Mrs. Volner added, "Why don't we all go into the living room?"

Mr. Volner put his arm around Veronica's shoulder as he followed her out of the entryway, but Veronica shook it off. Giving her a strange look, Mr. Volner shoved his hands into his pockets and made his way over to the couch. Veronica sat on the settee across from him, but she wouldn't look her father in the eye.

"Do you want some coffee?" Mrs. Volner asked, as if by rote.

"No thanks, Jill. I won't be staying that long. I just wanted to tell you my news, and I thought it might be good if the two of you were together."

He was going to tell her last week, Veronica thought. After the way she had acted at the antiques show, he must have decided it would be easier to do it with her mother there. Well, she'd show him. Veronica turned a dark gaze in his direction.

Mr. Volner cleared his throat. "So," he began, "I'm going to get married. That is, Sandy and I are going to get married. We haven't set a date, but we'd like to do it in the spring when Alex gets back."

The silence that followed lasted only a few seconds, but to Veronica it seemed like an eternity. Mrs. Volner broke it by saying, "Congratulations, Neal."

Mr. Volner seemed relieved at her response. "Thank you, Jill." Then he turned to Veronica. "Aren't you going to congratulate your old dad, too?"

Veronica wouldn't give him the satisfaction of that. She sat there stone-faced and turned her attention to the cold fireplace.

"Come on, Veronica. I was hoping for a few good wishes." There was a hearty note in his voice, but when Veronica gave him a sidelong glance, she was pleased to see him looking worried.

"Give her a little time, Neal," Mrs. Volner said quietly.

"You don't have to give me any time," Veronica burst out. "I don't like Sandy, and I think the idea of you two getting married stinks." Feeling the dampness starting to form behind her eyes again, she got up and hurried toward her bedroom.

Veronica flung herself down on the bed and let the tears come in earnest now. Despite her noisy crying, she listened for the sound of her father's footsteps in the hall. Maybe he would come in and tell her it was all a big mistake. Instead, after her sobbing had subsided, Mrs. Volner appeared in her bedroom. "Your father's gone," she said. "He was disappointed in your reaction."

"Who cares?" Veronica said in a muffled voice.

Mrs. Volner gently pushed Veronica over and sat down on the edge of the bed. "This is something you're going to have to get used to, Veronica." As if reading her mind, she added, "He's not going to change his plans."

Veronica brushed the tears out of her eyes. "He might."

Her mother slowly shook her head. "I don't think so."

"Has he told Alex yet?"

"He's going to call him."

"Alex won't care that much," Veronica said bitterly. "He's been mad at Daddy for so long."

"That's not a very healthy situation, either."

"I think Alex is smart. He wrote Daddy off years ago. I wish I had."

"He's your father, Veronica. And he isn't doing such a terrible thing. He just wants to be happy."

"Then he can be happy without me."

They stayed together for quite a while, silently. When the doorbell rang, both of them were startled.

"Who's that?" Mrs. Volner asked.

Veronica groaned. "Gretchen and Bobby

were going to come over and work on our project."

"Oh. Well, if you said you were going to study, maybe you should."

"I don't want to," Veronica said stubbornly. The doorbell chimed again.

"Veronica, you can't just stay up here crying all day. Get your mind on something else."

"All right, all right. Just let me wash my face with cold water."

Veronica kept a washcloth on her face, but when she looked in the mirror, it was still red and puffy. Only her mother's knock at the door brought her out of the bathroom.

"Veronica, here's Gretchen. Why don't you work up here?"

Veronica didn't say anything, but Mrs. Volner disappeared anyway, leaving Gretchen in the hallway. It was apparent Gretchen could feel the tension in the air. She looked embarrassed to be in the middle of something, and Veronica despised her for sensing that.

"Bobby called me," Gretchen said, following Veronica into her room. "He's sick."

"Then we shouldn't even bother working," Veronica snapped. "Why did you come here?"

Gretchen studied the floral wallpaper. "I started my report on the different kinds of writing—you know, fiction and nonfiction, and technical writing. I talked to my mom, too."

"Well, I haven't done anything yet," Veronica said defiantly.

"Oh, great." Gretchen shook her head.

Suddenly, Veronica had an overwhelming desire to make Gretchen feel as bad as she did. "I got some news today. You'll probably get the same kind eventually. My dad's getting remarried."

Gretchen stared at her blankly. Veronica wanted to slap her across the face.

"Better start thinking about what will happen when your mom or dad tells you that they're hooking up with someone else."

"I told you, that's not going to happen," Gretchen said stubbornly.

"Sure it is. That's why your parents aren't living together."

"You don't know what you're talking about." Gretchen started to look a little sick.

"They'll probably start a new family, too. Maybe give you a little half brother or sister," Veronica could hear her voice rising.

Gretchen turned shakily away, but Veronica caught her arm.

"And maybe they'll do better in the kid department this time around. Babies don't start out as geeks, do they?" To her disgust, Veronica could feel her eyes spilling over with tears.

"Just because you're so upset, don't call me names," Gretchen said, breathing hard. "This isn't my fault."

Suddenly, Veronica realized how vulnerable she was. How could she have let Gretchen see her like this? "You didn't see me upset," Veronica replied, wiping her eyes with the back of her hand.

"What are you talking about?"

"And you didn't hear about my father's remarriage." Veronica's words rushed out.

"I couldn't care less that your father's getting married." Gretchen's voice was shaking. "I came over to work, but I'll just tell Bobby you weren't prepared, as usual."

"Fine. Who cares? Get out of here."

Gretchen had already turned and was headed down the staircase.

"If I find out you've told anyone anything, you're going to be very sorry, Gretchen. Got that?" Veronica screamed down the stairs.

But the only reply was the sound of the front door opening and slamming shut.

CHAPTER
SIX

By the time Monday rolled around, Veronica had formulated a plan.

The fight with Gretchen had shaken her up, and she worried that Gretchen might tell everyone how upset she had been, just for spite. In the end, though, she convinced herself that Gretchen would keep her mouth shut. She had gotten on the wrong side of Veronica before and knew that wasn't a very pleasant place to be.

Just in case, however, Veronica decided to put out her side of the story first. In this new, improved version, Veronica was going to say she was thrilled about the wedding and adored Sandy. If Gretchen Hubbard tried to tell anyone differently, no one would believe her.

Her campaign began at lunch on Monday. Waiting until there was a lull in the conversation that already had covered Mrs. Volini's icky green blouse, the Wildcats' win last week, and Ham Berger's disgusting habit of cutting his fingernails and leaving them on his desk, Veronica very casually gave her tablemates the news.

"By the way, my father is getting married," she informed them.

"Married?" Candy squealed. "To Sandy?"

"Of course."

Candy had heard the good things Veronica had to say about Sandy, but she also knew how attached Veronica was to her father. "Are you happy about it?" she asked sympathetically.

Veronica laughed. "Of course. Why wouldn't I be?"

Candy fumbled for a response. "You don't know her all that well, do you?"

"Oh, she's cool. I got to know her better when we were at the ski lodge. It's kind of neat to have your father dating someone young for a change."

"Is it?" Natalie asked doubtfully.

Kim took a bite of her pizza. "I think it would be weird. Parents should be, well, they should be parent age."

"Sandy isn't going to be my parent, just my stepmother. And we'll probably be more like sisters." She smiled when she said it, though she was cringing inside.

"When are they getting married?" Lisa wanted to know.

"Sometime in the spring."

"Are you going to be a flower girl or something?" Candy asked.

"Oh, Candy." Veronica groaned. "A flower girl?"

"Well, or something, I said."

"A bridesmaid." Kim's eyes lit up. "That would be neat."

"I don't know. A bridesmaid at your own father's wedding?" Lisa made a face.

Veronica knew how to turn this around. "I'm going to have a great dress—something in silk, or a gauzy material. Off the shoulder, maybe. I'll have to start looking through those bride magazines."

Lisa, who particularly loved clothes, looked jealous. Kim turned to Natalie and said, "Some people have all the luck."

That was the response Veronica was waiting for. She breathed a small sigh of relief. No one would ever believe that she was unhappy about this stupid wedding now.

"Are they going to have a big wedding?" Candy asked, tearing off the wrapper of her Twinkies.

"Well, it is Sandy's first marriage," Veronica responded noncommittally.

"Maybe you could take some friends." Candy's expression was hopeful.

"I doubt it."

It would be hard enough to go to the wedding, without her friends hanging around.

"You could ask," Candy responded huffily.

"We'll see."

Fortunately, the conversation moved on to other weddings the girls had attended, and then it was time to go back to class. Veronica felt she had the situation under control, and with any luck, the topic wouldn't come up again for a while. She didn't relish the idea of pretending over and over again that she was thrilled by the idea of her father's remarriage.

As the girls hurried toward their classroom, Veronica caught sight of Gretchen. While she passed her, she gave her a stern glance that she hoped Gretchen understood. It meant, Keep your big mouth shut.

A long afternoon stretched ahead of Veronica when she got home from school. Helen was fixing dinner, and she asked Veronica whether she wanted a snack, but Veronica just shook her head and went up to her room.

Starting her homework seemed particularly unappealing and so did watching TV. Finally, she decided to write Alex a letter. They had missed their regular weekend call because Alex was on a ski trip in Switzerland. "Let's give your father time to tell Alex his news," Mrs. Volner had suggested. "We'll talk to him next week."

That didn't mean that Veronica couldn't write him. Mail to England was slow, and by the time he received her letter, he would, no doubt, have heard from their father.

Veronica pulled out the pink stationery edged with flowers that Robin had given her several Christmases ago and sat down at her desk to write. She had composed the letter over and over in her head, but now that she was faced with a blank page, she didn't know how to begin. Running her finger along the stationery, she had a funny thought. She wished she could talk to Robin. It would have been comforting to confide in someone who could look past her cover-ups and schemes and understand what was really going on with her.

Well, you can't, Veronica told herself firmly.

She began her letter.

Dear Alex,

I guess by now you've heard Daddy's big news. I'm sure he told you how great Sandy is. Believe me, she isn't. She hangs all over Daddy, and, like I told you, I don't think she's much older than you are. It's gross. Mom is pretty upset, too. I'm not sure why, because she's told me a couple of times that she doesn't love Daddy anymore, but then why should she care so much? Needless to say, things are grim around here. So what else is new? Daddy thinks I'm going to come around, but I'm not. I've already made it perfectly clear to him what I think of Sandy, and if she's not a total idiot, she's guessed, too. I suppose . . .

Veronica had heard the phone ring, but the words were coming more easily now, so she ignored it. However, when Helen appeared at the door and said, "Veronica, I've been calling up to you. Your dad's on the phone," she reluctantly put down her pen and picked up the phone next to her bed. Her heart was beating a little faster than normal, knowing that whatever her father was going to say to her wouldn't be pleasant. She wasn't looking forward to this conversation.

"Hello, Daddy," she said cautiously.

"I've been hanging on forever," her father began irritably.

"Sorry. I didn't hear Helen call me. I was writing Alex," she added significantly.

Her father got the message. "I guess you've been giving him your version of my engagement."

Veronica didn't say anything. Let him figure it out for himself.

"I talked to Alex this morning. He said he might come to our wedding."

That news wounded Veronica, but all she said was, "That's nice."

"Veronica, your mother suggested I give you a few days to get used to my news, but I have to tell you, I don't like the way you acted on Saturday."

She could feel all her angry feelings being stirred together. Sarcastically, she answered, "Sorry about that."

"Veronica!" Mr. Volner said sharply.

She wanted to show him she wasn't going to back down, but at the same time, Veronica hated to hear the harshness in his voice. "Well, what do you want me to do? Lie?" she asked, more subdued.

"Do you think you've given Sandy a fair chance?" her father countered.

She did, but she knew that wasn't the answer Mr. Volner was looking for.

"Sandy happens to be a lovely person who makes me very happy."

"She doesn't like me, either," Veronica muttered.

"That's not true. If you knew each other better, I'm sure you would get on together very well."

Oh right, Veronica thought.

For some reason, Mr. Volner took Veronica's silence for agreement. "That's what we'll do. We'll arrange for you two to spend a little time alone."

"Daddy." Veronica groaned.

"Veronica," Mr. Volner said seriously, "Sandy's going to be a part of your life for a long time to come. It will be better for everyone if you can become friends."

For you maybe, Veronica thought, not for me.

"Honey, I love you," Mr. Volner said. "I just want us all to be happy."

"I want that, too," Veronica finally replied.

"Well then, we'll all work toward that end. I'll talk to you soon."

Veronica hung up the phone and rolled over on her bed. Her father didn't get it. She was never going to like Sandy, no matter how much he wanted her to. It would be nice if they all could be happy, but with Sandy in the picture, that was never going to happen.

"Veronica," Mrs. Volner said that evening as they were sitting down to supper, "have you decided what you're going to do for your birthday?"

"I want a party—a boy-girl party."

A frown crossed Mrs. Volner's face. "You just had one at Halloween."

Veronica couldn't believe that her mother was offering the same objection as Mrs. Dahl. She had thought her mother was a lot cooler than that.

"That was months ago," Veronica said carefully.

"I would rather it was just girls," Mrs. Volner said as she cut her meat loaf into small pieces.

Veronica pushed her plate away from her. "Then I don't want to have any party at all."

Mrs. Volner didn't look at her daughter. "That will be all right, too."

Why was everything so horrible lately? She looked down at her plate, where the gravy on her meat loaf was beginning to congeal. Her mother must have read her mind, because she said in a soft voice, "Try to go with the flow sometimes, Veronica."

"What does that mean?"

"Don't fight things so much."

"Now you sound like Daddy." Briefly, she told her mother about her conversation with her father.

"He's right. You and Sandy should spend some time alone."

"Why are you sticking up for them?" an outraged Veronica asked. "I know you're not happy about this, either."

Mrs. Volner swallowed a piece of meat loaf. "Because I'm going with the flow."

As Veronica dressed for school the next day, she decided that maybe having a boy-girl party for her birthday wasn't such a good idea, after all. Billy hadn't been showing much interest in her lately, and Veronica was struck by the awful thought that he might turn her down if she asked him to come. That would be so humiliating, it was better not even to take the chance. She'd plan some spectacular party, just for the girls. They would be impressed, and her mother would be happy. It seemed like the safer way to go.

Veronica checked herself out in the mirror. The new blue sweater with multicolored bows all over it looked great with her jeans. She rummaged around in her jewelry box and found two blue barrettes that she used to pull back her hair. After one more glance at herself, she hurried downstairs, gathered her books, and slipped on her jacket.

As she got on the bus, she immediately noticed Robin and Gretchen sitting together, deep in conversation. Robin saw her as she passed and averted her head. Was that a guilty look on Robin's face, Veronica wondered, or was she just being paranoid?

The thought of Robin and Gretchen huddled together on the bus bothered Veronica all day. Don't be silly, she told herself. They could have been talking about anything. And Gretchen had been warned. Knowing there could be consequences, she wouldn't tell her secrets to Robin.

Library was the last period of the day. Most of the kids liked it. Unless they had special projects to work on, they were allowed to roam the media center and find books to check out. Miss Morris, the librarian, was remarkably good-natured and didn't seem to mind if there was a little noise, as long as some serious book choosing went on as well.

Some of the girls were paging through the most recent addition to their favorite paperback series, but Veronica wasn't interested. She already had bought her own copy at the bookstore. Leaving her friends arguing over who would get the library's only copy, Veronica made her way down the aisles. She was looking for a copy of *The Lion, the Witch and the Wardrobe.* Her mother had read it to her first when she was about seven, and it was still her favorite book, the one she always wanted to read if she was feeling sad or upset.

She recognized their voices before she saw them. Robin's whisper always had a husky quality that made her sound as if she had a cold. Gretchen was trying to keep her voice down, but she wasn't doing a very good job of it. Though she could only glimpse them through the bookshelves, Veronica could hear their conversation clearly.

"She was so upset," Gretchen was saying. "I didn't believe Veronica could be that upset about anything."

"Her dad was always really important to her. If anything would get to Veronica, it would be something like this."

Veronica could feel her face grow hot, though she wasn't sure whether it was from anger or embarrassment. How dare they discuss her personal affairs like this? And that pitying quality in Robin's voice—Veronica hated it.

"The weird thing was, even though Veronica was being so rotten, I ended up feeling sorry for her."

"Veronica can be horrible. Believe me, I know," Robin said with a sigh. "But I feel sorry for her, too. I remember how she felt when her parents got divorced."

"I think our project is in trouble, too. The person she's supposed to interview is her father's girlfriend, and I know she hasn't done it."

"That figures."

"I don't know what she'll do if she finds out I told you." Gretchen sounded really nervous.

"I'm certainly not going to tell her," Robin assured her.

Veronica had heard enough. Furiously, she went around the corner of the bookshelves and planted herself in front of Gretchen and Robin.

She was pleased to see how scared they looked.

"But are you going to tell anyone else, Robin?" Veronica demanded.

Robin stared at her silently.

"Cat got your tongue?" Veronica taunted.

"Veronica—"

Veronica cut her off. "I warned you not to say anything, Gretchen."

"I know, but I just—"

"She thought I could help," Robin interjected.

"I don't need any help," Veronica said flatly.

"I think you do."

"Well, I don't."

"Veronica, I know you don't want your dad to get married." Robin took a breath. "But he's going to do it anyway. You might as well just get used to it."

"Go with the flow?" Veronica asked sarcastically.

Robin blinked. "Yes."

"I don't feel like it, and I don't need any advice from you, thanks anyway."

"Fine," Robin said sharply. Veronica could tell that she was starting to get mad now, but she didn't care. She turned her attention to Gretchen. "As for you, Gretchen Hubbard, you're going to be very sorry that you opened your big, fat mouth. That's a promise." With that, she wheeled around and walked quickly away, her heart pounding. She'd show them, especially that stupid Gretchen. Nobody could mess with her like that and get away with it. *Nobody.*

C H A P T E R
SEVEN

Veronica wasn't sure why she was in the basement rummaging around through dirty old
cardboard boxes. If her mother found out,
she'd be mad—not just because Veronica was
making a mess but because of her mission. She
had been in her room trying to come up with
a plan to get back at Gretchen when suddenly
she had the overwhelming desire to look at her
parents' wedding album.

The white leather album used to be in the
bookcase of their family room. After the divorce, her mother had moved it down to the
basement along with their other photo albums.
It was as if getting those pictures out of sight
somehow would erase all those years together.

Veronica opened another box. This one contained her mother's high school and college yearbooks. She took out the one from Mrs. Volner's senior year in high school and turned to the graduation pictures. Listed under the name Jill Mathis was the quote, "The world is her oyster." A listing of activities followed: Cheerleading Squad, Drama Club, Honor Society.

Veronica stared at the smiling face, surprised at how young her mother looked and how much she looked like her—the same long dark hair and dark eyes. What really hurt, though, was the hopeful expression on her mother's face. This pretty girl probably had happy dreams of marriage and family. It scared Veronica to think that life could go so awry.

She shoved the yearbooks back in their box and began searching through other cartons. She found her own baby book and took a few minutes to leaf through it. It contained her baby bracelet from the hospital and all kinds of notations of firsts: her first smile, first word (Da Da), and, embarrassingly, the first time she had used a potty. Veronica lingered over a picture of her family. It was taken at a park. She was in her father's arms, and Mrs. Volner's hand rested on her husband's shoulder. Alex stood in front of them, his attention on a truck he was holding. Veronica slipped the picture out of the baby book and carefully tucked it into the pocket of her jeans.

She was about to try yet another box when she heard the phone ringing. Thinking it might be one of her friends, she rushed upstairs and caught the phone on the fourth ring. For a moment, she didn't recognize the voice on the other end.

"Veronica, I'm glad I caught you at home. Are you free this afternoon?" It was Sandy.

"Why?"

"I want to take you out to lunch."

Lunch with Sandy was the last thing she wanted to do. "I don't think I can."

"Why not?"

"My mother's not home," Veronica answered, thinking fast. "I'd have to ask her before I could do something like that."

"What time do you expect her?"

"I don't know," Veronica lied. Actually, Mrs. Volner should have been home by now.

"It's only eleven," Sandy said. "Why don't I call back in a half hour and check again. We'd still have plenty of time."

Veronica didn't see any way to avoid a second call. "All right," she finally answered.

Veronica was just hanging up the phone

121

when she heard her mother's key in the door. For a moment she considered not telling her about Sandy's invitation, but that only would be postponing the inevitable. Sandy obviously was not going to give up easily.

Mrs. Volner walked into the kitchen and put a bag of groceries down on the counter. "Veronica, there are a couple more bags out in the car. Will you help me bring them in?"

"Sure," Veronica said, but she lingered by the telephone. "Sandy just called."

"She did?" Mrs. Volner asked with surprise. "What did she want?"

Veronica made a face. "To take me out to lunch this afternoon."

Mrs. Volner busied herself putting away the groceries. Her face was hidden as she said, "That sounds like a good idea."

"Oh, Mom," Veronica groaned. "I don't want to."

Putting down the cans in her hand, Mrs. Volner turned to her daughter. "Veronica, you can't avoid Sandy for the rest of your life."

"I can if I try hard enough."

Mrs. Volner shook her head. "It might be nice to think so, but you know that's not true."

"But, Mommy, I don't want to." Veronica

almost never used that childish term anymore, but she was feeling awfully small.

Moving quickly to Veronica, Mrs. Volner took her in her arms and gave her a hug. That was another thing Veronica hardly ever tolerated, but right now she felt safe and protected in her mother's embrace.

"Let's go upstairs and find something nice for you to wear to lunch," Mrs. Volner whispered in her ear.

So, though it was against her will, Veronica found herself dressed and ready when Sandy came to pick her up an hour later. There was a terribly awkward moment when Sandy came into the house and introduced herself to Mrs. Volner.

Mrs. Volner, meet the future Mrs. Volner, Veronica thought to herself.

"I heard congratulations are in order."

"Thank you," Sandy replied.

"I hope you'll be very happy."

Veronica was proud of the way her mother was handling herself. Sandy looked uncomfortable, but Mrs. Volner seemed perfectly in control.

"Well, we should probably get going," Sandy said, turning to Veronica.

"I'm ready," Veronica said through tight lips.

When they were in the car, fastening their seat belts, Sandy turned to Veronica and asked politely, "Is there anyplace you'd like to go?"

"Not really."

"All right. Let's go to the Palace. I owe you a meal there."

"Fine." Veronica decided she was going to eat plenty. As long as Sandy was paying, she was going to take full advantage.

There was a chilly silence on the ride to the restaurant, but once they were seated and had placed their orders, Sandy turned to Veronica and plunged right in to the topic that was on both of their minds. "So, what are we going to do about our problem, Veronica?"

There was no use pretending she didn't know what Sandy was talking about. "I don't know."

Sandy leaned forward, her blue eyes intent. "I know your father has told you, but let me say it, too. We love each other very much."

Veronica traced a pattern along the edge of her napkin and didn't reply.

"We are going to get married. We hope you'll be happy for us, but if you're not . . ."

Sandy shrugged. "We'll get married anyway."

"I don't know what everyone wants from me," Veronica finally said, the words exploding from her lips. "It's like you want me to pretend to be happy, when I don't feel that way. People always tell you to be honest, so I am honest, and then you're disappointed because I tell the truth."

Sandy leaned back in her chair and looked at Veronica. After a moment, she said, "I see your point."

"You do?" Veronica asked, surprised.

"Sure."

Veronica hadn't expected any agreement with Sandy. How should she deal with it? she wondered.

Sandy gave her a slight smile, as though she could read her mind. "I guess you're surprised to hear me say that. But now that I think about it, you are getting some mixed messages from us."

"I'll say," Veronica muttered.

"Veronica, your father and I don't want you to lie; we just wish you could give us your blessing. I suppose, though, you had your own ideas about the way things would work out."

"What do you mean?"

"You wanted your parents to get back together."

Veronica refused to meet Sandy's eyes. "I suppose I did," Veronica finally said.

"That's understandable."

Veronica didn't like the way things were going. She decided it was time to bring out her big gun. Reaching into her purse, she pulled out the picture she had found in the basement that morning and pushed it toward Sandy. "See what a happy family we used to be."

Sandy picked up the picture and studied it. "You were just a little baby when this picture was taken."

"So?" Veronica asked defensively. "We had plenty of good times together."

Sandy's blue eyes grew serious. "It might have seemed that way to you, Veronica, but your dad tells me that he and your mother were unhappy for a very long time."

Veronica didn't want to admit anything to Sandy, but she had talked to Alex a lot about this subject when he was home. He had told her that late at night he used to hear their parents arguing. "Just because they had some problems doesn't mean that they couldn't work them out someday."

"You know, Veronica, my parents were divorced, too."

"They were?" Veronica hadn't been expecting that.

"I had many of the same feelings you do, but now that I'm grown up, I know that my parents never would have gotten back together, even if they both hadn't remarried. It's very unusual for divorced couples to remarry."

Before Veronica could respond, the waitress came with her club sandwich, fries, and milk shake. She wasn't a bit hungry now. When the waitress finally left, Veronica hoped that they could change the subject. She could see that she wasn't going to get anywhere with Sandy, who was so full of good arguments. Maybe now would be the time to bring up the subject of that stupid interview she was supposed to do. Even though she tried not to think about her assignment, the deadline was growing close, and her lack of work was beginning to gnaw at her. Talking about the assignment would change the subject, anyway. However, Sandy wasn't quite done with it. As soon as the waitress disappeared, Sandy said, "So, are you going to continue this vendetta against our marriage?"

"What's a vendetta?" Veronica was sure she had a pretty good idea of what the word meant, but she was stalling for time.

"A campaign. In this case, a campaign to make everyone as unhappy as possible."

Veronica had to say one thing for Sandy. She certainly didn't pull any punches. "Do you still want me to be honest?" she asked, equally bluntly.

"I guess so."

"I don't know what I'm going to do." Veronica hoped that would get a rise out of Sandy, but she just nodded.

"Fair enough, but remember, Veronica, keep this up and the person who will come out hurting the most is you."

Before Veronica could argue, Sandy started talking about several of the new movies she had seen, and even though Veronica didn't add much to the conversation, it didn't seem to faze Sandy at all. In fact, Sandy seemed more cheerful than ever. She got happier still when Veronica finally told her about Career Day and asked to interview her for the project, even though Veronica didn't make her request very nicely. "We're having Career Day at school, and I got stuck with doing a project on writers and writing."

"Really?" Sandy raised one eyebrow.

"It wasn't my idea," Veronica added hurriedly. "But my teacher found out I knew someone who was a writer and she said I had to interview you." That should show Sandy how she felt about the subject.

"I'm sorry you got stuck with writers," Sandy said, "but, of course, I'd love to talk to you about what I do. Shall we talk now?"

"I'm too tired now." Veronica was telling the truth. She felt as if she had just run a marathon.

"Then let's make it soon."

"We have to," Veronica responded sourly. "Our reports are due in a week or so."

When Sandy dropped Veronica off, she said, "I enjoyed our lunch together."

"You did?" asked Veronica with surprise.

"I think we made some progress."

Veronica pondered this. Then she said, "You didn't convince me of anything."

"But at least we both know where we stand," Sandy said pleasantly.

Veronica could feel her mood growing blacker all afternoon. She had given her mother the briefest possible report about her lunch and then had gone up to her room and shut the door. Veronica tried to take a nap, but whenever she nodded off, Sandy's smiling face punctuated her dreams.

Though her room was dark, Veronica could see the glowing numbers on her digital clock. It was after five. There was no point in trying to sleep anymore. Besides, she should get up and do her homework. At least she could work on her report and chart about famous writers. On Friday, Bobby had asked—demanded, really—that it be ready the next time they all got together to work.

"Otherwise, I might have to tell Mrs. Volini you're goofing off."

"What?" she had asked, outraged.

"Gretchen and I were talking about it. You know, part of the grade is on what we do together. We don't want you to screw things up for us."

Veronica had just stared at Bobby. She was a good student, hardly the kind that screwed up.

"I know you haven't done your interview. What about the stuff you were going to do about famous writers?"

"Don't worry, Bobby. It's practically done."

She sat up in bed. All she knew about famous writers was in a few notes she had taken from the encyclopedia. She hadn't bothered to read the biographies. Everything was spinning out of control. Suddenly, she had a thought that calmed her. There was one situation she could do something about: getting even with Gretchen Hubbard.

Every time she thought about Gretchen, Veronica could feel the anger rise in her throat, an ugly, sour taste. Gretchen with her big mouth. Prissy Gretchen, who had announced to Mrs. Volini, during a discussion of Career Day, that her interview with her mother was all finished. Maybe her father and Sandy were beyond her reach, but Gretchen was another matter. Gretchen she could handle.

Veronica went downstairs to find her mother, who was watching television in the den.

"Do you want to see this nature show?" Mrs. Volner asked. "It's just starting."

"No," Veronica said, sitting down beside her. "Can I have a sleepover tonight?"

Mrs. Volner swiveled around to look at her. "It's a little late, isn't it?"

"Well, I could just call some of the girls."

"Oh Veronica . . ." Her mother groaned.

"Please."

Mrs. Volner looked at her daughter. "All right," she said, giving in with a sigh. "I guess you've had a rough day. You deserve a little fun."

"Thanks, Mom," Veronica said, leaning over and giving her a kiss. "You're the best."

"For the moment," Mrs. Volner said, directing her attention back to the television.

Veronica hurried to the phone and started calling her friends. Candy, Kim, and Natalie were all available.

When the girls arrived, Veronica made popcorn and took them down to the rec room. "I have an idea," she said as they got settled.

"What?" Candy asked with interest.

"It's about Gretchen. She's being such a jerk. I hate working with her."

"Ohh," Candy squealed. "You said you'd get even with her for not backing off the project. I wish she would have, too. I wound up interviewing a man across the street who sells real estate."

Veronica saw no need to enlighten the girls about her real reason for making trouble for Gretchen. She had a ready-made excuse in the project, and she might as well use it to her best advantage.

Natalie reached over for a handful of the popcorn. "Are you going to make her screw up on the oral report?"

"If I did that, it might affect my grade, too," Veronica replied, fingering her hair.

"You wouldn't want that," Kim said dryly.

Veronica turned and gave Kim a fierce look. "Do you want to be part of this or not?"

Kim shrugged. "Sometimes these plans of yours don't work out, Veronica."

Veronica could feel herself flush. She knew Kim was referring to the time, after the fight with Robin, that she had turned the girls against their former friend. In the end, though, she was the one who had come out looking bad.

"Fine," Veronica snapped. "Then I'll do this one myself."

Natalie punched Kim in the arm. "Come on, Kimmy, don't be such a jerk. Since when do you take Gretchen's side over Veronica's?"

"Besides," Candy said, washing down the popcorn with a sip of Coke, "Gretchen thinks she's so great now. I heard her telling Robin and Sharon that when she lost five more pounds, her father said she could get a whole bunch of new clothes. She really thinks she's going to be some glamour queen or something."

Veronica saw Natalie and Kim exchange shrewd glances. Everyone knew that Candy was afraid of Gretchen winding up thinner than she was. Candy's remark had given Veronica an idea, though.

"Maybe Gretchen does think she's turning into a hot number," Veronica said thoughtfully.

"Come on," Kim scoffed. "Gretchen Hippopotamus?"

"And maybe we can encourage her in her little fantasy," Veronica continued.

Natalie looked at her curiously. "What are you talking about?"

"Gretchen is probably interested in knocking off some weight because of boys, right?"

Natalie shrugged. "I suppose."

"Well," Veronica said, her smile growing. She paused to build up suspense. "What if we make her think that some boy is just crazy about the new, improved Gretchen?"

Candy started to giggle. But Kim asked, "How are you going to do that?"

"We could start by leaving her a note," Veronica said, warming to her plan.

Natalie clasped her hands in front of her, " 'Oh, darling, please be mine,' " she beseeched.

Veronica laughed but shook her head. "No, dopey, she'd never believe that. But she might go for something like, 'Gretchen, I'm a little shy, but I like you very much.' "

Kim ran over to the desk in the corner of the rec room and got a pencil and a piece of paper. "We should start writing this down."

"Good idea," Veronica said approvingly.

"Who's supposed to be sending these notes?" Candy asked.

"Well, at first it will be a mystery." Veronica was improvising.

"Gruesome Gretchen and the mystery man." Natalie laughed. "How romantic."

"But who knows? We may come up with a boyfriend for her."

"Ham Berger," Kim suggested. "He's pretty gross."

"Or Luke the Puke," Natalie suggested, still giggling. Luke was the nerdiest boy in the fifth grade.

"And by that time, Gretchen will think

she has a real secret admirer." Veronica gloated.

"Wait until she finds out the only boyfriend she has is us," Natalie said.

Right, Veronica thought. That will teach her.

C H A P T E R
EIGHT

"Let me see it," Lisa demanded.

The girls were standing outside Mrs. Volini's room, waiting for the first bell to ring. Veronica and the others had filled Lisa and Jessica in about their plan to make Gretchen think she had a secret admirer. Before falling asleep Saturday night, they had even written the first note to slip in her desk. Lisa and Jessica were sorry to have missed the fun, but they were eager to see how the scheme would work.

Veronica reached into her pocket and pulled out the crumpled piece of white paper. "Now, don't let anyone see you," she said, looking around the crowded hallway.

"This is pretty messy," Lisa commented as she opened the smudged note.

"It's supposed to be from a boy," Natalie pointed out.

" 'Dear Gretchen,' " Lisa read. " 'I've been watching you for a long time. I think you're pretty cute. Your secret admirer.' "

"That's it?" Jessica asked, disappointed.

"That's it for now," Veronica corrected. "We're going to send more notes, remember. Besides, if it was too enthusiastic, she wouldn't even believe it."

"We wrote a couple of really good ones on Saturday night," Kim said with a giggle. " 'My darling Gretchen, I can't live without you. I don't know what I'll do if you won't be my girlfriend.' "

"You're right," Lisa agreed, "she never would have bought that."

"After that, we got a little silly," Veronica said. "What was that one you came up with, Candy?"

" 'Dear Gretchen, dear, I love you. You've got my most important qualification for a girlfriend—a big chest.' " Candy barely could choke out the words.

"I wrote a poem: 'Gretchen, you're fetchin'. They call you a fatty, but you drive me batty.' " Natalie was proud of her effort.

"Boy, I wish I had been there." Jessica laughed.

"So who's going to put this in her desk?" Lisa wanted to know.

"We thought you would," Veronica said.

"Me?"

"Well, you do sit right across from her."

"But what if she sees me?"

"I'll keep her busy talking about our report. Candy can stand lookout."

"Here she comes," Kim said, pointing down the hall.

"All right." Lisa snatched the note out of her hand. "But where exactly should I put it? Her desk is so messy. If I just stick it in there, she might not find it for a week."

"Put it in her math book. We have math first. Now hurry," Veronica hissed. "She's coming."

Lisa scurried away, and Candy went to her assigned lookout post. As Gretchen came closer, Veronica told Jessica, Natalie, and Kim to leave, too.

"But why?" a disappointed Kim asked.

"It'll be less suspicious if I'm by myself." Veronica turned away from the retreating girls and maneuvered herself in front of Gretchen, barring the way as she tried to get to the door. "Hi, Gretchen."

Gretchen looked at her warily.

"I arranged to interview my writer."

"Good," Gretchen said, trying to step around her.

"Once it's done, you, me, and Bobby should get together."

"I suppose we have to," Gretchen said, facing Veronica.

Veronica turned her head and saw Candy discreetly nodding at her. Lisa must have finished her errand. "I can't wait," she said, turning her back on Gretchen.

As the bell started ringing, Gretchen followed Veronica into the room. Lisa was already sitting in her seat, as was Candy. Veronica waited impatiently as Mrs. Volini took attendance and read off the day's announcements. "Now, remember," she said, "your Career Day reports will begin a week from today. Is everyone ready?"

There were a few bored nods, which sent Mt. Volini into a boil. "I expect a little more enthusiasm, class. You should have learned all sorts of intriguing things about your subjects by now." She turned her gaze on Jonathan.

"Jonathan Rossi, what have you found out about the teaching profession?"

A stricken Jonathan glanced over at Robin. "Well, you can teach in grammar school or high school or college," he began hesitantly. "And you can teach all kinds of subjects."

"Yes, Jonathan, I believe we all know that." Mrs. Volini frowned. "Tell us the most interesting thing you learned."

"If you want to make a lot of money, don't go into teaching."

The class burst out in laughter.

"I'm sure you can do a little better than that, Jonathan," Mrs. Volini said pointedly. "All right, take out your math books."

Lisa had strategically placed the note right at the beginning of Chapter Eight, the chapter the sixth grade was supposed to begin today. Gretchen couldn't help but see it as she opened her book.

Carefully plucking it out of its hiding place, Gretchen unfolded the piece of paper and read it. Veronica watched with satisfaction as Gretchen flushed and looked quickly around the room. Then she shoved the note in her desk.

Veronica waited impatiently until lunchtime, when she and her friends had gathered at their usual table. "Did you see her?" she asked as soon as everyone was seated.

"Yes," Lisa said. "She fell for it, hook, line, and sinker."

Natalie and Jessica, who were both in Mr. Jacobs's room, bemoaned the fact that they had missed it. "How did she look?" Natalie asked.

"Thrilled," Lisa said promptly.

"She patted her hair," Candy added.

"Did she?" Veronica laughed. "I missed that."

"Oh yes," Candy assured her. "She was getting all ready to meet the new man in her life."

"What now?" Kim wanted to know.

"Another note," Veronica said quickly.

"When should we do it?" Jessica asked. "This afternoon?"

"Not that soon," Veronica replied. "Let's give her a little time to try and figure out just who her dream man is."

In the end, the girls decided to wait until the next day to give Gretchen the second note. They couldn't bear to put it off much longer than that.

"What should it say?" Lisa wondered.

"Well, I think Mr. Secret Admirer should

tell Gretchen he wants to go out with her. It's the next logical step. A big step for a big girl," Veronica added, amidst a gale of giggles.

Veronica arrived home that afternoon, still trying to think up just the right phrases for Gretchen's next note. She barely said hello to Helen, but she snapped to attention when the housekeeper stopped her ironing to tell her that she had a letter from Alex.

"Where is it?"

"Put it on your desk, where I always stick your mail."

Veronica hurried upstairs to her room, where the distinctive blue airmail letter with its foreign stamp was waiting.

She ripped it open and quickly scanned the letter. Then she settled in her rocking chair to read more thoroughly what Alex had to say.

Dad called and told me about the happy event. He wants me to be at the wedding, since he's waiting until I get home. Maybe I'll go; I'm not sure yet. It would be easier for everyone if I did, I guess. I'm sorry you don't like Sandy. I suppose I'm not going to care for her much, either, but, like I've been saying for years, it's his life. I know it hasn't been that simple for you, Veronica.

143

You've got to remember, though, that if you want to see Dad, she's part of the package now, too. Take them or leave them, but either way, it's got to be both.

Veronica could feel the tears forming behind her eyes. She had expected more from Alex. That was his advice, take them or leave them? Alex was telling her, it seemed, if she wanted Dad, she was going to have to get used to Sandy. Thanks a lot, Alex, she thought. Even he was letting her down.

It struck her that until these last few moments she had spent almost a whole day, the first in a long time, without thinking about her father and Sandy. It had been very pleasant not to have them cluttering up her mind. Maybe that was the secret, just to ignore them altogether.

Veronica pushed the letter into her desk and picked up a pencil. It was time to write another note to Gretchen. At that moment, Lisa called, asking whether she wanted to come over.

"Sure, Lisa," Veronica said. "I was just going to write Gretchen a note. We can do it together."

"Good. I was sorry I missed out over the weekend."

Veronica informed Helen that she would be back before dinner, then hurried outside. Lisa lived on the other side of Rosewell Park, a pleasant area with a large playground and a duck pond that would be frozen over until spring. It wasn't a short walk, but the weather had warmed up a little.

She was halfway across the park when she noticed Billy coming toward her. His lack of attention was still a sore spot with Veronica, but since it didn't seem as if they could avoid each other, Veronica was willing to give him one more chance.

"Hi, Billy," she said.

"Hi, Veronica."

They stood there silently for a second or two. Then Veronica, putting on her haughtiest expression, said, "Guess you've been busy."

"Busy?"

Veronica hated having to explain herself, but finally she said, "I haven't heard from you in a long time."

Billy frowned. "So?"

"Oh, never mind," Veronica snapped, and then she turned to walk away.

"Wait. I get it. 'Cause we went to the dance, right? You thought we were going to start dating or something?"

Veronica wanted to cover her ears. Instead, she just kept moving.

"It was just one dance," he called.

"Maybe to you," Veronica muttered when she was well out of earshot. Suddenly cold, she stuck her hands into her pockets. She was humiliated, but she was also angry. That Billy Page had a heck of a lot of nerve. In her own mind, she and Billy had been a duo. Now, it was pretty clear they weren't.

Then she had a worse thought. She had made the mistake of implying to her girlfriends that Billy really liked her. Veronica wondered just how she was going to explain that he didn't.

Veronica pondered that problem the rest of the way to Lisa's house. She hadn't come up with any solution by the time she rang the doorbell.

"What's wrong?" Lisa asked curiously after she let Veronica inside.

Suddenly, Veronica had an idea. "I just had a fight with Billy."

"Where did you see him?" Lisa seemed startled by the news.

146

"In the park."

"What did you fight about?" she demanded as they sat down on the couch.

Veronica decided she had better be vague. "He just started acting creepy."

Lisa's interest was piqued. "So you don't like him anymore?"

"No, I don't," Veronica said emphatically. "And I told him so."

"Well, that's good, I guess." Lisa was uncertain. "He's awfully cute, though."

"He's very immature."

Lisa nodded. "Don't worry. My mom says boys are like buses. Another one always comes along."

Veronica wrinkled her nose. She didn't think boys were like buses, but all she said was, "There have got to be better guys than Billy Page."

"Gretchen must be dreaming about her wonderful new boyfriend right now," Lisa said with a sly smile.

Veronica grinned back. "I bet you're right."

"So what are we going to write in this note? We've got to make her think someone is hot for her bod."

"That bod? It won't be easy."

"It's got to be believable," Lisa warned.

Veronica leaned back against the couch and thought for a moment. "Maybe we should lay off the compliments. Just write and say he wants to get together."

Lisa's eyes sparkled. "That's good."

"Yeah, a date."

"Then what will happen?"

"He won't show up, of course."

"But she might just think he got shy," Lisa objected.

"That's true." A scheme began threading itself through Veronica's mind. Maybe there was a way to get back at Gretchen and Billy at the same time. "What about this," she began slowly. "First, we send her a note saying he'd like to get to know her better. Now she's really anxious to find out who this guy is. Then, we send her another one saying he wants to meet her at The Hut."

Lisa was confused. "But no one will be there."

"Oh yes there will. Billy will be there."

"Billy!"

Veronica shaped her plan as she explained it to Lisa. "We send Billy a note, too—a really hot note. Something like, 'Billy, I think you're so great. I'm a fan of yours. I wish you'd meet me at The Hut and later we can have some real fun.' "

Lisa clasped her hands in front of her. " 'Oh, Billy, darling, you're such a hunk.' "

" 'I'm a hunk, too,' " Veronica said in a high, silly voice. " 'A hunk of blubber.' "

The girls started laughing so hard they could barely catch their breath.

"Too bad she's lost some weight," Lisa finally said. "She was a whale."

"She's still fat enough."

"So, Billy will see it's Gretchen and—"

"He'll throw up," Veronica interjected. "He'll also be really embarrassed."

"So will Gretchen."

"She will be when Billy turns around and walks away from her." Veronica could see it all now: Billy, walking into The Hut thinking some awesome girl is dying for him. Gretchen, sitting there, excited, thinking she's going to meet her secret admirer. She almost faints when she finds out it's Billy, and then almost dies when he turns his back on her. Billy leaves The Hut cringing because he's been suckered into a meeting with Gretchen Hubbard.

A perfect scenario. Just perfect.

C H A P T E R
NINE

Veronica was happy to see that everything was going according to plan. Yesterday morning, Gretchen had received her second note. Short and sweet, all it said was, "Gretchen, I like you a lot. You're looking good."

The girls had had a big laugh when they saw Gretchen and Robin studying the message at lunchtime.

"I wonder who she thinks her lover boy is," Kim said.

"She's sure going to be surprised when she finds out it's Billy." Natalie tried to look discreetly in Gretchen's direction.

The girls had been surprised when they found out that Veronica had—as she put it— dumped Billy. Much to Veronica's relief, though, they had unquestioningly bought her story.

Now, however, Lisa said, "Are you sure you want to go ahead with bringing Billy in on this?"

"Why not?" Veronica asked with an edge to her voice.

"Well, you might want him back someday, and if he ever finds out you were behind this . . ."

"He's pretty awesome," Candy said with a small sigh.

"He's a drip." Veronica was definite. She did feel a pang as she dismissed him, however.

"Like my mother always says . . ." Lisa began philosophically.

To keep Lisa from getting started on boys and buses, Veronica said, "Now, have we decided how we're going to get the note to Billy tomorrow?"

There was a heated discussion as to how to go about it. They could try to stick the note in one of his books, or maybe in his locker. Finally, they decided that Jessica, who was also in Mr. Jacobs's room, would just put it on Billy's desk when she had the chance.

"You know, he might not go to The Hut," Lisa warned. "He could just blow off the note."

Veronica was prepared for this possibility. "I suppose, but I'm counting on the fact that Billy thinks he's so great, he'll go just to check it out."

"When he sees who it is, he might turn around and leave," Natalie said.

"He could, but Gretchen will be waiting, and she'll see that disappointed look on his face. And if she doesn't figure it out for herself, I may go over and explain the whole thing to her."

"Would you?" Lisa asked, her eyes wide.

"Sure," Veronica replied flippantly. "I haven't gone to all this trouble just to have Gretchen think her boyfriend got shy."

Veronica was pleased to see the awed looks on the faces of her friends. She knew she had more guts than any of them. She was glad that they knew it, too.

After school, Veronica decided to stop downtown and buy some new barrettes. Her mother had told her at breakfast that she was going to be working late that night, and Veronica wanted to avoid going home as long as possible. There was something about eating dinner alone that always made Veronica feel especially sad. In those television shows, reruns of "The Waltons" or "Father Knows

Best," the whole family sat around the dinner table together every night. Even when her parents were married, Veronica didn't remember many meals like that. Either her father was working late or Alex had some kind of practice to go to and her mother had to drive him there. Veronica was the only person who was always home at dinnertime.

Before she and Robin had their bustup, Veronica would have called and asked whether she could eat over at the Millers'. Mrs. Miller was a good cook and didn't seem to mind Veronica's joining them. In some ways, Veronica missed Robin's family just as much as she missed Robin.

Veronica walked into the boutique where she was going to buy her barrettes. The first person she saw was Robin, standing in front of a display of bracelets. Maybe because she was thinking about her, Veronica wasn't surprised. And almost as if she sensed her presence, Robin looked up as Veronica stood hesitantly in the doorway.

Robin had been examining a bangle. She went back to what she was doing for a second or two, then put it down and walked over to Veronica, just as she was about to turn and leave.

"Veronica, I have to talk to you," Robin said.

"What about?"

"Not here. Let's go to the deli."

Both girls were silent as they walked across the street to the brightly lighted deli. There were a couple of empty booths, but the girls sat at the counter, where they could just get Cokes without the waitress frowning at them.

"So, what did you want to talk about?" Veronica asked uncomfortably. Even though there was no possible way Robin could know she was responsible for the notes to Gretchen, Veronica felt guilty. Robin always had the uncanny ability of guessing what was on her mind. Veronica wondered whether she was still in practice.

Taking a sip of her Coke, Robin began. "I've been wanting to talk to you since that day in the library."

Veronica stiffened. Suddenly, she didn't feel quite as guilty.

"Anyway," Robin continued, "you shouldn't have gotten so mad. After that scene at your house, how could you expect Gretchen just to keep quiet?"

"She was broadcasting my problems all over the library."

"She was just talking to me, off in a corner."

"I heard you, didn't I? I could have been anybody."

"Okay," Robin conceded, "maybe that's true. But remember, Gretchen understands what you're going through. She's pretty unhappy about her own parents."

Veronica didn't say anything. Whatever was happening with Gretchen couldn't be nearly as miserable as her own situation.

"Besides," Robin continued, "I'm glad she told me."

Veronica looked at Robin contemptuously. "Why? What do you care?"

Like a lot of redheads, Robin could get mad quickly. She flushed as she said, "Maybe I don't. But we were friends for a long time. I thought . . . oh, never mind." Robin put her head down and determinedly sipped her drink.

"Thought what?"

Robin ignored her for a minute. Then finally she looked at Veronica and said, "I thought maybe I could help. But I don't want to help you. You're such a creep."

Veronica felt a little dizzy. She had never thought of herself as a creep. She knew some of the things she did weren't very nice, but it was because people deserved them, or because she was forced into it. Veronica hated it, but she felt as if she might start crying any second.

Robin must have sensed the tears because her voice softened as she said, "You don't have to make other people unhappy when you're miserable."

"I don't. I don't do that."

Robin shook her head. "Oh, Veronica, you do so. You couldn't stand it when it turned out Jonathan liked me, so you made sure you got back at me. It's what you always do. You have a mean streak a mile wide."

"Since when did you get so holy?" Veronica asked heatedly. "We were best friends. You were right there beside me when I was planning things."

"I guess I was." Robin paused. "I even thought a lot of what you did was funny, until you did it to me."

Veronica slid off her stool. She reached into her pocket and threw a dollar on the counter. "Here, this is for my Coke."

Robin pushed the money back at her. "I'll pay."

"Fine." Veronica grabbed her dollar back.

Without a backward glance, she rushed out the door.

A blast of cold air hit Veronica, but it felt good against her hot face. She hurried home, bitterly going over the conversation again and again. "A creep," Veronica muttered. If anyone was the creep, it was Robin Miller.

Tomorrow, at least, Robin's pal Gretchen would get hers. Then Veronica would find some suitable punishment for Robin. Suddenly, a feeling of overwhelming weariness enveloped her. It was hard to keep thinking up things to do to people.

Veronica opened the front door, expecting to find an empty house. Instead, Mrs. Volner was in the kitchen.

"I thought you were going to be late," Veronica said, hoping that her mother wouldn't notice how upset she was.

"I finished early." Her mother peered at her. "Are you all right?"

"Sure," Veronica said as she hung up her coat. Mothers must have some sort of radar. Half the time, it seemed as if Mrs. Volner wasn't paying any attention to her at all, but the minute things were going wrong, her mom was suddenly all ears and eyes.

Mrs. Volner set out the tuna casserole that

Helen had left for them. She was peering into the refrigerator as she said, "I'm going to the movies tonight."

"You are?" Veronica asked, surprised. "Can I come, too?"

Mrs. Volner straightened up. "No. Your father and Sandy are coming over tonight."

"Here!"

"Yes, here," Mrs. Volner said flatly. "Your dad called me at work and made the arrangements."

The tears that had been threatening since her talk with Robin were about to spill over. "How could you let them come over?"

"They want to talk to you about their wedding plans."

"No," Veronica shouted. "No way. I don't want to know anything about their stupid plans." She turned to flee, but her mother grabbed her by the arm. Veronica struggled for a minute, and then she let her mother sit her on a chair. "I guess I'm not going with the flow," Veronica finally said with a trembling smile.

"No way." Mrs. Volner brushed away a tear on Veronica's cheek. "What do you think we ought to do about that?"

Veronica shrugged. "I don't know."

"I suggest you start by washing up, and then having supper. You'll feel better after you eat."

Veronica doubted that, but she did as her mother said. As she helped herself to some of the casserole, she asked, "Did Daddy tell you anything about his wedding plans?"

Mrs. Volner shook her head. "No. And I didn't think it was my place to ask."

"What time is he coming?"

"In about a half hour," Mrs. Volner replied, checking her watch.

"I'll be ready, I guess," Veronica said with a sigh.

"So how was the rest of your day?"

She pushed away the memory of her fight with Robin. "Oh, okay."

"You want to talk about it?" her mother asked shrewdly.

For once, Veronica did, but she didn't know how or where to start. "I had a fight with Robin."

"Robin? I haven't heard you mention her name in a long time."

Veronica had given Mrs. Volner an abbreviated and none-too-accurate version of her troubles with Robin when they were happening.

Mrs. Volner had approved of Robin, and she had urged Veronica to work out their differences, until it was obvious that wasn't going to happen. Eventually, she had accepted the fact that Veronica and Robin were no longer the inseparable friends they once had been. Now her mother said, "Is this a continuation of your old fight or a new one?"

"Both, sort of."

"What happened?"

Veronica sat up. She didn't know how much she wanted to divulge, but there was one thing she needed to find out. "You don't think I'm a creep, do you?"

"Is that what Robin called you?"

"Yes," Veronica muttered.

"She must have had her reasons."

"Mom!"

"We both know Robin's not the kind of girl who just goes around calling people names."

"So you think she's right," Veronica said accusingly.

"I don't know anything about the circumstances," Mrs. Volner pointed out.

Veronica really didn't want to describe them, either. All she wanted was reassurance from her mother, but she wasn't getting that.

Normally, this would have made her furious. Now, it just made her sad. "It doesn't matter," Veronica said.

"It certainly does."

"Well, I don't want to talk about it anymore." Veronica pushed away her plate. "I suppose I'd better get ready for Daddy."

Mrs. Volner looked as if she wanted to continue their conversation, but all she said was, "Maybe you should." Then she added, "But if you want to talk about this again, let me know."

"I will," Veronica said, but she promised herself she wouldn't say another word on the topic of Robin.

Mrs. Volner timed it perfectly. She was walking out the door to go to her movie just as Mr. Volner and Sandy were driving up. Mrs. Volner threw them a wave before hurrying to her car. Veronica was left to usher them into the living room.

"So how are you, Veronica?" Sandy asked. She looked particularly nice today in a bright blue sweater with pants that matched. She also looked very happy.

"I'm fine."

Mr. Volner was making himself comfortable

on the couch. "Did your mom tell you Sandy and I wanted to talk about our wedding plans?"

"Yes."

Mr. Volner and Sandy exchanged glances. "It's not going to be a big wedding," Sandy began, "but I think it will be lovely. We're going to have it at a little church in the city."

Veronica didn't know what to say. Hearing about her father's wedding was weird.

"We'd like you to be a bridesmaid," Sandy continued.

"A bridesmaid?" So what she had suggested to the girls was really happening.

"Yes, Sandy and I both think it would be nice if you were in the wedding party."

Veronica looked down at her hands. She didn't want to be in the wedding. She didn't even want to attend, but she knew she'd probably be forced into it. A number of responses ran through her mind—things such as "I wouldn't be caught dead at your wedding" or "I'd rather be anywhere else." But Veronica knew how she would feel if she uttered any of those thoughts—like a creep.

"Veronica?" her father said questioningly. "Would you be in our wedding?"

"I guess so."

"Good!" Sandy said. "Let's get together

soon and look for dresses." She seemed genuinely happy and Mr. Volner was beaming.

Veronica was far from happy, but she comforted herself with the thought that for the moment, anyway, she didn't feel like a creep.

C H A P T E R

TEN

Veronica watched from her desk as Gretchen read her note for the fourth time that morning.

The first time she'd looked at it, a big smile had spread over her face. She quickly began scribbling a note to Robin, who looked surprised but pleased when she read it.

Gretchen had tucked the piece of paper in her purse, but she had pulled it out during English, and then again while Mrs. Volini was talking about a field trip to the Museum of Natural History in Chicago that was coming up next week. As the sixth grade was putting their books away for lunch, Gretchen opened up the now-worn piece of paper to read it again.

Veronica was surprised to find herself feeling worse each time she saw Gretchen with the note in her hand. Where was the satisfaction she usually experienced when a plan of hers was working out well? In its place was a kind of dread. Veronica wasn't looking forward to going to The Hut and watching Gretchen get her comeuppance.

She tried to argue with herself. Gretchen deserved this. Hadn't she blabbed about Veronica's most private emotions? However, each time Veronica tried to muster up some anger, she remembered how Robin and Gretchen had sounded in the corner of the library. She had hated the pity in their voices, but she knew they weren't making fun of her. She also remembered Robin saying that Gretchen understood how it felt when your parents were messing up your life.

Well, it was too late to do anything about it now. When the girls arrived in the lunchroom, Jessica already was sitting at their table with a satisfied look on her face. "It's all taken care of," she informed her friends as soon as they sat down.

"He got the note?" Candy asked eagerly.

"Yep. I put it on his desk right before he came in, and he was grinning when he read it. He even passed it over to Roy Higgins. He'll be there," Jessica said confidently.

The other girls looked excited, but Veronica felt even worse than she had that morning. She was reminded of a time when she was much younger. She had just learned to ride her bike and had made the mistake of attempting to ride down a steep hill. The bike had careened wildly out of control. The same sick, scary feeling was with her now.

She tried to cover it up. "I guess both of them are in for quite a surprise—a bad one."

"Where are we going to be?" Candy wanted to know.

"Yeah," Lisa chimed in. "Won't Gretchen be suspicious when she sees us all there?"

Natalie came up with what she termed a brilliant plan. "We don't go in right away. We wait outside until we see Billy, then we go inside right before he does. See, that way, we get to see the whole thing, but Gretchen doesn't get suspicious."

The others agreed it was a great scheme.

As the afternoon progressed, the sick feeling in Veronica's stomach only got worse. She couldn't figure it out, and she kept telling herself the whole episode would be funny. But watching Gretchen enthusiastically singing away during music, Veronica knew it wouldn't be funny at all.

She toyed with a drastic idea. Maybe she could warn Gretchen, tell her not to go to The Hut. It would mean confessing the whole scheme. But how could she possibly tell Gretchen what was going on without the girls finding out? And what would they think of her then? No, the scheme had gone too far for her to back out now.

After school, Veronica dutifully went downtown with Lisa, Jessica, Candy, Natalie, and Kim. Normally, she would be the one leading the laughing and giggling. Now, she tried hard to keep a smile on her face while the others joked about the romantic encounter that was about to take place.

It was too cold to stand outside. The girls crowded into the drugstore across the street, where they could look out the plate-glass window and watch everyone who came in and out of The Hut. It didn't take long for Gretchen to appear—and Robin was with her.

Veronica's stomachache immediately got worse. She had assumed that Gretchen would be alone. Robin, Veronica knew, would catch on to her treachery far more quickly.

The other girls didn't see it that way, of course.

"She's going to be really embarrassed because Robin's there," Candy enthused. She turned to Veronica. "Isn't that great?"

"Yeah, great."

They only had to wait a few minutes before Billy came walking up the block. Gretchen knew from her note that her mystery man was tall and would be wearing a leather jacket. Billy's note said to look for a girl with blond hair, a navy sweater, and a green down jacket. They had added that bit of information after they checked out what Gretchen was wearing. There was no way those two were going to miss each other.

"Come on," Lisa said. "Let's go get a table inside." Scurrying across the street, the girls managed to race inside before Billy got near the door.

Gretchen didn't see them, but Robin looked at the girls oddly as they noisily took a table where they could have a good view of the proceedings.

They had barely gotten themselves settled when Billy walked in. He looked around the room curiously, his eyes first lighting on Lisa and then Candy, both of whom were blondes. Since neither was wearing the proper clothing, he continued to glance around The Hut.

Meanwhile, Gretchen had spotted Billy with his leather jacket. When it was obvious he, too, was looking for someone, Gretchen's eyes grew wide. She jabbed Robin, who began to frown.

It took Billy a few seconds, but finally he focused on Gretchen, the disappointed expression on his face was obvious for anyone who cared to see it. He turned around to leave, but then hesitated. Resolutely, he made his way to Gretchen's table. The girls were close enough to hear the conversation, if they listened hard.

"Did you write me a note?" he asked gruffly.

Gretchen was not expecting this. "Did I write . . . ?"

"Yes." He pulled the note from his jacket pocket and shoved it at her.

Barely glancing at it, Gretchen said softly, "I'm the one who's been getting notes—from a boy. He said he was going to meet me here."

"Well, it wasn't me," Billy said emphatically.

There was a confused silence. Then Robin said, "I think somebody's been playing a joke on you guys." She glanced over at the girls' table. "Or a couple of somebodies."

Billy didn't stop to figure out who Robin was

talking about. "Some joke," he said with disgust, before wheeling around and quickly making for the door.

The girls nudged each other under the table, and Candy had to put her hand over her mouth to hold in her laughter. Only Veronica was quiet, feeling Robin's eyes boring into her.

"What should we do now?" Kim asked.

"Veronica, are you going to go over and say something to Gretchen?" Lisa wanted to know.

Not in a million years, she thought. Before she could phrase that in some way that wouldn't arouse suspicion, she looked up and saw Robin marching toward their table.

"Maybe we should get out of here," Veronica hissed. She didn't have a chance to get up, though, because Robin was standing in front of her.

Ignoring the other girls, Robin said, "Veronica, you're behind this, right?"

Veronica tried to look innocent.

"Behind what?"

"You arranged this whole stupid stunt, didn't you?"

"Why would she do that?" Candy asked.

Veronica shot Candy a "shut up" look, but it was too late.

"Why? Because she said she was going to get back at Gretchen for blabbing about her big secret."

Now it was the girls' turn to stare at Veronica. "Secret? What secret?" Lisa asked.

"She's probably told you how happy she is about her dad getting remarried, right?"

There were a few nods.

"Well, she hates the idea," Robin said emphatically. "She was crying the afternoon she found out. She told Gretchen she was miserable about the whole idea. Then she warned Gretchen that she better never tell anyone else."

"Shut up," Veronica whispered. "Just shut up."

"But Veronica likes Sandy," Candy said with confusion.

"Oh no, she doesn't. She can't stand her, and when she overheard Gretchen telling me what had happened, she promised Gretchen would be sorry. This is her payback." Robin stood there, solidly planted, breathing heavily.

The girls didn't know what to say. Lisa was moving her finger around a scratch in the table, while Kim and Natalie looked at Veronica in disbelief. Jessica was shaking her head.

Only Candy still seemed unsure about what to believe.

The silence was broken by Robin. "That's the real story," she said. Then, she turned and went back to Gretchen, who looked just as dismayed as Veronica's friends.

When she was gone, Lisa asked, "Is that true, Veronica? You always told us how great Sandy was and how happy you were about your dad's plans."

"Why did you even bother to lie about it?" Kim asked quizzically.

"You . . . you wouldn't understand." Veronica pushed away from the table and got up in one quick motion. "Never mind. Just never mind."

Veronica was not quite sure how she got home. She supposed she walked, but she didn't remember anything about it. She was too busy replaying the awful events of the afternoon, over and over, to pay any attention.

When she walked through the door, the phone was ringing. Helen, who was vacuuming the living room, called, "Veronica, get that, will you?"

No, Veronica wanted to shout, but the telephone was insistent. "All right," she shouted over the vacuum cleaner's whine.

"Hello?"

"Veronica, it's Sandy. I was wondering, could you come with me tonight when I look for wedding dresses? There's a bridal shop at the mall near your house. We could check out something for you to wear, too."

"Why do we have to do it so soon?" Veronica asked. Her heart was pounding. "There's plenty of time."

There was a silence on the other end of the line, and then Sandy said, "I'd appreciate it if you would reconsider. Dresses have to be ordered and fitted, and I'm about to go out of town on business. We could do your interview, too. You still have that assignment, don't you?"

Veronica was too tired and upset to argue. It would be hard to make this day much worse anyway, and Sandy was right. If she didn't do something about her stupid assignment, she'd be in even more trouble than she was now, if that was possible. "All right, if my mother says it's okay."

"Fine. Unless I hear from you, I'll pick you up about seven."

Veronica barely had put the phone back on the hook when it rang again. This time, it was someone else Veronica didn't want to hear from—Lisa.

"What is it, Lisa?" Veronica asked wearily.

"I'm at my house with Kim and Natalie. We want to get some things straight. What Robin said was true, right?"

"Yes, it's true." Veronica was tired of lying.

"But why didn't you tell us you didn't like Sandy? We're your friends."

Why hadn't she? Looking back, all the stories seemed so stupid now. "I don't know."

"Gretchen deserved what she got for telling Robin your secret," Lisa said slowly. "It's just that you didn't give us the real reason."

Veronica didn't know how to explain that Gretchen really didn't deserve the trick. "Gretchen wasn't telling to be mean."

"Oh no?" Lisa scoffed.

There was no way for Veronica to answer.

"Well, we're not mad at you," Lisa said. "But you should have told us the truth."

The truth, Veronica thought as she hung up and went upstairs. She tried to remember the last time she had told her friends the truth about anything.

Veronica sat at her desk for a long time wondering what she should do next. She thought about writing Alex, but she had the feeling he wouldn't understand her actions, either. Veronica was almost relieved when Helen stuck her head in the door.

"Your mom called."

"Yeah, I heard the phone ring. What did she want?"

"Working late."

"Oh." She didn't know if she would confide in her mother, but she did wish they could spend the evening together. She guessed she'd go with Sandy. "I'd better call her and tell her I'm supposed to go out with Sandy tonight."

Her mother was harried when Veronica finally got through, and she immediately gave her consent to the evening's plans.

Although she hadn't been looking forward to the outing, by seven o'clock Veronica was longing to get out of the house and away from her thoughts. Sandy's excitement was evident as she drove them to the bridal shop in the mall.

"I've got the caterer for the reception." Sandy was bubbly. "We'll have hot hors d'oeuvres—shrimp puffs and little stuffed mushrooms. . . ." She noticed that Veronica wasn't paying much attention. "I guess you're not very interested," she said crisply.

"No, I am." Actually, she was. She was grateful for any distraction.

Sandy looked at her curiously. "You want to hear more about our plans?"

"Sure." Veronica tried to keep up her end of the conversation. "How many bridesmaids are you having?"

"I thought you knew. Just you."

"I'm the only one?" Veronica couldn't have been more surprised.

"Well, I don't have that many close friends, and your father is going to ask Alex to be his best man. I thought it would be nice if we could all stand up there together."

"Like a family," Veronica said flatly.

"No. Like four people who are embarking on a new relationship."

When Sandy put it like that, it didn't sound quite as bad. "What kind of a dress do you want?" Veronica asked.

"I'm not sure." She smiled. "But I can't wait to start looking."

They certainly saw a lot of dresses, but Veronica didn't mind. Despite her misgivings about the wedding, Veronica had to admit it was fun seeing all those white and ivory confections that Sandy tried on. She found herself getting into a festive mood despite herself, and she was even happier when it was her turn to try on dresses.

"But what about you?" Veronica protested. "You haven't decided yet."

"I'm going to look downtown tomorrow. I have to make a decision soon. I kind of like that sleeveless one. With the beaded neck?"

"It was pretty," Veronica agreed. And Sandy looked beautiful in it, though she didn't mention that.

"Now," Sandy said, turning to the saleslady, who was hanging up dresses, "what about our bridesmaid here?"

The woman questioned them both a little about color, and Sandy and Veronica decided they wanted something in blue. It didn't take long for her to come back with armfuls of blue—azure, sapphire, turquoise. Veronica and Sandy looked at each other and started to laugh.

The woman looked slightly offended.

"I'm sorry," Sandy said, getting control of herself. "I just never realized there were so many shades of blue."

It took a few tries, but finally Veronica put on a deep-blue silk dress that looked wonderful on her.

"Well, we'll take this, don't you think, Veronica?"

"Oh yes!" Veronica exclaimed. She loved the way she looked in it.

While the dress was being wrapped, Veronica realized that for a little while she had been happy. How weird to think that the reason for her good feelings was the dreaded wedding. Now that the excitement of trying on dresses was over, however, Veronica could feel herself being enveloped again by a dark cloud. Her change of mood was so obvious that Sandy couldn't help but notice it.

On the way home, she said, "Is there something wrong, Veronica? I thought we were having a pretty good time in there."

Veronica's irritation with Sandy washed back over her. Why couldn't she just leave her alone? Sandy was not to be dissuaded easily, however.

"Was it something I said?"

"No. It doesn't have anything to do with you."

"Something at school?"

When Veronica didn't answer, Sandy said, "I can make a pretty good listener, but I don't want to push you."

Something in Sandy's tone made Veronica

say, "A couple of girls at school are mad at me."

Sandy turned her eyes from the road and looked at Veronica. "Oh?"

"Well, they sort of have a reason to be. I pulled a trick on one of them."

"Do you want to tell me what you did?"

"No."

"But it was bad?"

"Yes."

"Did she deserve it?"

That was a funny question, Veronica thought, and one that endeared Sandy to her. It made her feel as if Sandy understood how things worked. She had to answer honestly, though. "I thought so, but now I don't."

"Then you're not going to feel better until you make it up to her."

"That's what I was afraid of," Veronica said with a sigh.

"You know how people say that when you do something bad, you're only hurting yourself?"

"Yeah."

"Sometimes that's true, Veronica. If you've treated this girl badly, and you know it, it will hurt you more than it will ever hurt her if you don't make things right."

Veronica was silent for the rest of the ride home. She hated to admit it, but she had to agree with Sandy. No matter how awful Gretchen was feeling about this afternoon, Veronica was sure that nobody could feel worse about it than she did.

C H A P T E R
ELEVEN

"What time should I pick you up?" Mrs. Volner asked as she drove along.

About five minutes after you drop me off, Veronica wanted to say. This was the moment she had been dreading, being alone with Gretchen. Of course, Bobby was going to be there, too. They were meeting at his house, after all. Even with Bobby present, Veronica had the distinct feeling it was going to seem as if she and Gretchen were the only ones there.

Veronica had taken the easy way out. She had stayed home from school on Friday, saying she had a stomachache. It was no lie. Her stomach really did hurt. But it wasn't from anything she had eaten, as she had implied to her mother.

She curled up in bed all day and did nothing but watch soap operas and eat the meager breakfast and lunch that Helen brought up on a tray. It took a lot of effort, but Veronica had managed to avoid thinking about events at The Hut. Every time Gretchen or Robin popped into her mind, she just concentrated on the television screen, where the people in the soap operas seemed to have almost as many problems as she did.

After school, however, the telephone rang shrilly, and though Veronica thought about not answering it, her curiosity won out.

"Hello?" she said cautiously.

"Hi, Veronica." It was Candy. "I can't believe you didn't come to school today."

"I'm sick."

Not even Candy believed that. "Sure. Anyway, everybody was talking about what happened to Gretchen."

"How did they find out?"

"Well, I guess we told a couple of people."

Great, Veronica thought.

"And Gretchen and Robin must have told some people their version of the story. Then people started asking Billy what happened."

Veronica leaned back against her pillow. What a mess! "So now everyone knows?"

Candy paused. "Everyone knows parts of it, but there are some pretty weird stories going around."

"Like what?"

"I heard some people say that Billy had gone over to your house and yelled at you. That didn't happen, did it?"

"No."

"Some people are on your side, and some people are on Gretchen's."

Veronica closed her eyes. "I wish everybody would just forget about this."

"I don't think that's going to happen, at least not for a while."

Veronica thought that for once in her life, Candy was probably right.

Although she was getting bored lying in bed, Veronica spun out her illness into Saturday. The one thing she did do was call Sandy and finally conduct her interview over the phone. To her surprise, some of the things Sandy told her about being a writer were interesting.

Veronica thought that writing was pretty easy. All you did was sit down and the words just came. Sandy had a different view. She talked about all the research a writer had to do before she ever got around to putting words on paper. And she described what it felt like to have writer's block, when it seemed as if you'd never put a sentence together again.

When she got off the phone, Veronica had a funny thought. If she had met Sandy in any other context, she might have liked her. If she were a teacher or a friend of her mother's, for instance, she would have thought Sandy was a pretty neat person, someone who was smart and funny, too. Was it only because Mr. Volner loved Sandy that Veronica hated her?

Once Veronica had finished writing up her interview, she knew that she should make arrangements with the rest of her committee for a final meeting. Bobby had pestered her about it on Thursday, but Veronica had been way too busy worrying about Gretchen's rendezvous with Billy to give any thought to a stupid oral report.

She wondered if there was any way out of getting together with Gretchen and Bobby. She was trying to think up a good excuse when Bobby called.

"Veronica, I don't care what you did, even though it was lousy. We still need one last meeting."

"Bobby, I don't think Gretchen would want—"

"I already talked to Gretchen. She doesn't care if you're there."

"She doesn't?"

"Nope. She said all she cares about is getting a good grade."

That didn't leave Veronica much room for protest. "All right. Do you want to come here?"

"No, my house. Neutral territory."

Any minute now, Veronica was going to be face-to-face with Gretchen. She wasn't sure how to act. All she knew was, she wished she could be somewhere else.

"Oh, hi," Bobby said as he opened the door. "She isn't here yet," he added shrewdly.

Veronica threw him a withering look.

Leading her into the den, Bobby continued, "You girls! You're always pulling something on each other. Why do you do that?"

Veronica pondered the question for a moment. It was a reasonable one. "I don't know," she finally said. "Gretchen was such an easy target, I guess. It was so simple to make her feel bad, we couldn't resist."

Bobby shook his head as he sat down. "She didn't seem that upset on Friday. She said the trick made *you* look like a jerk, not her."

"Gretchen said that?" Veronica wondered whether Robin had coached her with that line. It didn't sound much like Gretchen.

When Gretchen arrived, however, the first thing Veronica noticed was the resolve on her face. There was a new determination in her voice, too, as she told Bobby, "I want to talk to Veronica for a minute before we get started."

Bobby practically jumped out of his chair. He obviously didn't want to be a witness to what might happen next. "Sure, no problem," he said as he left the room.

Veronica knew, even on Friday when she was home in bed, that she was eventually going to have to apologize to Gretchen. She wanted to do it now and get it over with, but before she could say anything, Gretchen spoke.

"You sure went to a lot of trouble just to get even with me. Did you enjoy it?"

"Not really."

"Me, either."

"I'm sorry," Veronica said, forcing out the words. "Things just got out of hand."

"Things always get out of hand with you, Veronica."

Now Veronica was starting to get mad.

Gretchen had her apology, what more did she want?

"Everybody is getting really tired of you."

"What are you talking about?"

"You should have heard what people were saying to me yesterday. They all have their own stories about what a creep you are."

Creep. There was that word again. Veronica didn't feel any better hearing it the second time around.

"Remember when you told me if I turned a cartwheel in front of the gym class, you would let me into your club? You apologized to me for that, but you didn't really mean it, did you?"

"Probably not," Veronica admitted.

"So why should I believe you this time?"

Veronica shrugged.

"I don't care if you're sorry or not, Veronica." Gretchen gave her a steady look. "Maybe you'll always find ways to make fun of me, but I don't care what you do anymore. If I keep losing weight, someday I'll be as thin as anyone else. But you're always going to be mean, and I don't think you can ever change."

There was a long silence. Veronica hoped she didn't look as ashamed as she felt. Finally, she said, "Look, Gretchen, do you want to finish this report or not?"

"That's why I'm here." Gretchen called Bobby into the room.

He looked warily at both girls. "Ready to start?"

"We're not going to pull each other's hair out, Bobby, if that's what you're worried about." Veronica said this in what she hoped was a calm voice.

"Well, that's something." Bobby pulled out his chart showing the history of writing. "All right," he said, "after our introductions, we can start with this."

They were all uncomfortable at first. Veronica kept stealing glances at Gretchen, who refused to look at her. She tried to keep her mind on the topic of writers, but it wasn't easy.

"So you'll do the famous-writers thing after me? Veronica?" Bobby snapped his fingers in front of her face.

"I heard you. Yes, I'll talk after you."

"I'll go next with my interview," Gretchen said.

They spent the rest of the afternoon tying up loose ends. The whole time, though, what Veronica really wanted to do was push Bobby out of the room and corner Gretchen. She wanted to get mad at her, and she wanted to ask her exactly what kind of stories the other kids had told her. Mostly, though, she wanted to tell Gretchen she really was sorry.

Instead, Veronica sat quietly, taking notes. When her mother came to pick her up, she just said good-bye.

Veronica was quiet on the way home.

"Cat got your tongue?" her mother teased.

Veronica thought about confiding in her mother but decided against it. She had the feeling her mother wouldn't understand. To her surprise, she realized that Sandy was a better sounding board than her mother. Maybe it was because Sandy was closer in age to girls who were nasty just for the fun of it.

She and her mother ate dinner in front of the television set, but Veronica couldn't concentrate on the show. "I think I'll go to bed early," she said as she took her empty plate to the kitchen.

"Still feeling under the weather?" Mrs. Volner asked sympathetically.

"I've felt better."

When she got upstairs, Veronica sat in her rocker and thought about the people she wished she could talk to right now. Alex was one. Yet, being a guy, he probably wouldn't understand any more than Bobby had. She wished she could talk to Robin, too. But Robin was probably lost to her. She knew what her friends—Lisa or Kim or Candy—would say. They'd tell her she was taking the whole thing too seriously, that the prank they had pulled on Gretchen was funny.

Veronica rocked silently back and forth. They'd be wrong, though. If she had learned anything from this whole stupid affair, and from her problems with Sandy and her father, it was that hurting people wasn't much fun— not for the other person and not for you.

Unbidden, Gretchen's words came back to her: "You're always going to be mean, and I don't think you can ever change." For a long time Veronica rocked, wondering if Gretchen was right. Would she ever change?

She looked out her window, where a shimmering of snow was starting to fall. It touched the yard and the trees, making the whole outside look different. Change herself—that was a scary idea. Until now, she hadn't wanted to.

Maybe I can, she thought.